D1522004

NORTH END
The Black Forest

AMANDA TURNER

DEDICATION

For Lola and Wilco - Thank you for being so cute.
For Adam - Thank you for making all of my dreams come true.

CONTENTS

1   North End   1

2   Fireflies   26

3   Weekly Consultations   47

4   The First Victim   65

5   A Suspect   87

6   Up All Night   110

7   A New Normal   121

8   Level-Headed   152

9   Losing My Family   168

10   Hallow's Eve   180

11   A Night to Remember   196

12   The Black Forest   215

13   Salvation   227

14   Safe and Sound   246

15   Winter Break   256

About the Author   268

1
NORTH END

I *looked around while my eyes adjusted to the light. It was early morning, the sun just rising, peeking above the trees. The air was cold, and I could see my breath blending with the fog. My eyes adjusted, but my brain didn't register where I was yet. I'd been here before. It was familiar. I looked down. My feet were planted on dirt. There were a few old, brown leaves leftover from fall, but the ground was mostly bare. I looked to my left. All I could see were unbelievably tall trees extending forever into the sky. And fog. It was so thick I couldn't make out anything further than a few steps ahead of me. I gazed above. The sky was dimly lit, and snow was falling down on my head. I was in the forest. But why? I couldn't remember what brought me here. I took a few steps to my left. Maybe I could find someone. Or find my way out, but the fog was so thick it was dangerous. I could easily get lost. No one would find me out here.*

I tried to move, but it felt like my feet were in mud. I looked down again to check, but I was still on the bare ground. There was no mud. I willed my legs to move and they finally did. As I trudged forward slowly, very slowly, I began to make out a figure a few feet ahead. The figure was dressed in a dark cloak. I couldn't tell if I knew them. The face was hidden by the cloak.

"Hello?" my voice echoed, vibrating off the trees. No response. I heard something loud in the distance. It was shrill and pierced through the air, echoing like my voice had, but amplified. I turned to my right and realized the forest edge was so close. Beyond it was the school. My school. My home. The walls were crumbling, engulfed in deep red flames...

I woke up to realize I was literally jumping in my sleep. I had startled myself awake. I felt confused and groggy for a moment. The dream, or nightmare really, was still on my mind and I couldn't remember where I actually was. It was pitch black around me, but my mind placed me in my childhood room. That couldn't be right. I saw the tall, black curtains covering the long windows on the side of my room, and it clicked into place. I knew where I was. It was impossible to tell if anyone else was still asleep. Lillian slept in the bed directly beside mine, but even her bed was covered in a blanket of darkness. The only thing I could see was the clock on the wall opposite my bed. One sliver of sunlight peeked through the top of the curtains casting a light on the ancient, yet giant, wall clock. *6:39. On no*! I slung the covers off my bed and jumped

NORTH END: THE BLACK FOREST

up. I landed on the cold concrete. The frigid surface stung my feet, and I jumped back on my bed in shock, which was a good thing because my head was dizzy from standing up too fast.

Once my head stopped whirling, I stood up again, slowly this time, and walked over to the curtains. I opened them carefully so just a few rays of light shone in the room. It was enough to see that the three other beds in the room were empty. Everyone else was already up. *"Why didn't Lillian wake me?"* I thought to myself angrily, cursing under my breath as I walked to my closet. The rational side of my brain knew it was *my* fault I overslept since *I* was the one who must have forgotten to set my alarm last night, but it was easier to secretly fault someone else for now, until I was fully awake and conscious enough to accept blame where it was due. I grabbed my bathroom bag from the top shelf of my closet and scurried out the door accidently slamming it behind me.

Normally I would have been awake at 5:45 a.m. so I could spend the first 30 minutes of my day eating breakfast and sipping tea on the front balcony of the school. There are several small tables on the balcony, as well as old rocking chairs. Students are allowed to spend evening free time and breakfast there. But at nighttime, the area was restricted for students. Which made me sad. It was the most beautiful view in the whole school, and I longed to see what it looked like with twinkling stars painting the sky.

Our school isn't your average boarding school. It certainly wouldn't look like a school to the outside eye, not that many outside eyes ever see this place anyway. We're located on a remote island off the coast of Ireland. And when I say "remote," I mean it. I never even knew the island existed until I stepped foot on it four years ago. It takes over three hours to arrive here by ferry, and there are no planes on or off the island. Access is restricted, as well. There is only one port on the island, and it is littered with security constantly. You cannot board the ferry on either side of the port if you are not a professor, student, or parent to a student of the school. Or unless you are a witch. A witch that has a confirmed appointment with another witch at the school.

Even if you knew of the remote island and spent your day and night kayaking to reach it, you wouldn't be able to make it onto land. All sides are covered in large, sharp rocks with waves thrashing against them constantly. As far as I knew, no one had ever tried to enter the island this way. And if they had, they were never heard from again. Even if the rocks didn't lead them to their demise, the residents of the island would. When you're on an island full of witches, it's hard to sneak anything past anyone. And no one liked surprise guests.

It was a shame for the outside world, the humans who had to miss the beauty of this island. It was all green. Everywhere you looked was grass or tall trees or ocean rocks covered in moss. The waves were visible from almost anywhere on the tiny island, which was only around one mile long. The waves were so high because our Headmistress placed a spell on them long ago. "They protect us," she explained to my class our first day on the island. The waves only calmed when a guard commanded them to do so, and the guards only commanded them to do so if they were expecting a planned arrival.

The trees were the tallest I had ever seen. Some would put the buildings in New York City to shame and the flat land allowed you to see them all crystal clearly. There were no hills. Where I grew up, there were rolling hills everywhere. I thought I would miss them. But I didn't. There was something about flat land, about being able to see as far as your eyes could reach, no matter which way you looked, that brought comfort, allure, and majesty to the island. I almost couldn't believe it was real the first time I stepped foot here because I didn't think it was possible for anything to be this beautiful.

Our school was a castle. It was impossibly old, from a different era entirely, but had been preserved by witches for centuries so not a stone was worn down. It even served as a safe haven for many witches when they were being hunted by humans during various witch trials around the world.

The castle, made of deep grey stone, remained in pristine condition. It was countless stories high and the grounds in total took up more than half the island. There was even a drawbridge that took you over a moat surrounding the castle. However, it hadn't been used in years since very few threats presented themselves to the school. Which made sense considering the most powerful witches resided inside. So, no one entered through the drawbridge. Instead, they entered through the castle barbican on the east side of the campus. It had all the trappings of a medieval castle, including a portcullis, ramparts, turrets and towers. There were even rumors that there were oubliettes, used to punish witches, somewhere hidden in the castle, but no student had ever actually seen them. When I was thirteen, experiencing my first year at the school, Lillian and I heard noises in the night. She would swear it was witches locked away in the cells, pleading for a chance at redemption.

Yes, it was a pity that most of the world would never see this tiny island and the unbelievable sights it held. Any human would take one look at it and be sure they were dreaming, like I had the first time I came here. It was nothing short of magical and the land showed that. All sorts of mysteries lurked on the island. Some darker than others.

I shuffled down the hall as quickly as I could since I was already late, and Professor Rose did *not* allow tardiness. She was one of the strictest professors at North End School. To be fair, every professor was pretty strict here. The rules were so rigid. They had to be. Young witches could *not* be given the chance to use their magic for anything but good. And if a student did try to use their magic for evil, they were quickly met with punishment from a professor—or worse, Headmistress Craw—that left them wishing they had never stepped out of line. Each one of the professors were among the strongest witches in the world, after all.

The school's main goal was focus. It's important for young witches to focus on their studies, focus on their spells, focus on their relationships with their fellow witches. When you have the ability to kill at the tip of your fingers, you must be taught what to do with it. How to control it. And how to use it for your will only. We weren't forced to use our magic for good when we left the school, but it was certainly encouraged. Although it was important to consider what *good* meant in our world versus the human world. But witches didn't follow the same rules as humans, even though some lived secretly among humans when they graduated.

I made my way to the bathroom with my burgundy robe brushing the ground. A strict dress code was one of the rules young witches were required to follow. We all wore clothing that was almost identical when attending classes. They varied in color depending on what year you were. This was my 4th year, therefore, at the moment I was dressed in burgundy pajama pants, with a button up silk shirt and a robe, which was optional. Unlike actually attending the school. Being a student here was an unspoken rule in the witch community. It didn't matter where you lived in the world or what coven you were from, who your parents were or how they decided to educate you before your 13th birthday. As long as they were known to the Headmistress, all young witches attended this school from ages 13-19.

There were some witches who blended into the modern world, choosing to live without their powers. Those who chose that life could live seemingly undetected, which meant they could not be forced to attend school at North End. That type of witch was called a "hitch" by most, meaning witches living as humans.

Hitches didn't follow the Divinity or the Fallen Angel and had turned their back on their magic. Most people in our world couldn't understand why they chose to live this way, but deep down I got it. They didn't ask for this. Perhaps they didn't want to move halfway around the world to attend a school where dangerous spells were taught regularly. I could understand that because a small part of me felt the same way. So, I didn't use terms like "hitch" in a derogatory way like most students, who used it as a hurtful word when they wanted to slander someone else's name. I just used it to describe what they were. Not an abomination. Just people who chose a different path in life.

It was easy for hitches to remain undiscovered for the entirety of their lives if they never had children. The longer they lived outside of this world, without using their powers, the quicker their magic faded away. Even if they chose to practice magic from time to time, they were difficult to track down. If they chose to have children, however, it complicated things. If a child discovered their magic and chose to act on it, the second they uttered their first spell, they could be traced. Only a witch's first use of magic is traceable. Even if the child lost control of their emotions, they could use magic without even meaning to. Because of this, hitches had to work hard to keep an extremely low profile. If they were found with a young witch and refused to send them to our school, the parents could be locked away or killed. My parents had described it as "magical negligence" once. They said it wasn't much different than giving a child a knife with no explanation on how to wield it.

So, if a child was found they would be forced to attend school at North End. The process seemed hypocritical to me, even after everyone's justifications. The witch community preached free will, but hardly ever practiced what they preached. They claimed witches could live their life as they pleased, then required them to attend this school. They claimed we could worship what we wanted, whether that be the Divinity, the Fallen Angel, or nothing at all, but any class that discussed a religion of sorts mostly focused on the Fallen Angel, or the devil as humans know him. I had a feeling that had to do with our Headmistress and her beliefs. Humans usually thought of the Fallen Angel as a villain in a scary story or a monster in their dreams. They're taught that the Underworld is a place of pain and somewhere you certainly wouldn't want to end up. But a lot of witches thought the exact opposite. They longed to be in the Underworld after their life was over. They weren't scared of the Fallen Angel. Instead, some worshipped him. I sided with the human world on this subject. The Underworld was not somewhere I ever wanted to step foot in.

The whole process of seeking out these hitches seemed unnecessary since those who chose not to attend school here didn't reap any of its benefits and therefore couldn't be considered a danger. If witches weren't taught any actual spells or how to use their powers properly, they eventually faded over time. And if they chose to only live in the mortal world, then they too would age like a mortal. That's another reason I believe this island is magical. If I had never stepped foot on it, I would have been just like any other human by the time I was 30. My powers would have dulled so much I would have been lucky if I could cast a simple charm, and my body would have begun weakening. But since I *did* step foot on the island, my powers would only grow stronger as I aged. And since my aging began slowing rapidly when I turned sixteen, it was unknown just how powerful a witch could become.

I sped past the stone walls of the hallways that were dim,

only lit by small torches at the top. They appeared every few feet. Witches loved darkness and I wasn't an exception to that particular rule. I was thankful the halls were dim in the mornings. It would not have been pleasant to wake up late and be blinded by bright fluorescent lights.

I made it to the bathroom and swung open the dark oak door that ran all the way to the ceiling. It was 6:40 and class started at 7:15, so I guess I was skipping the shower today. Heading straight for the mirror, I passed several of my classmates. Some were wrapped in towels, drying their hair, others were in front of their mirrors applying makeup, and a select few were just exiting the showers with wet hair, uncaring that they would undoubtedly be late for their first class. One of those brave few with soaking wet bodies was Frances.

I ducked my head as I passed the wall of showers and hoped the steam that filled the room was enough to hide me from her. I was not in the mood for a conversation. But, of course, the steam was not enough to mask my face. Frances stepped directly in front of me, confident, even though she was wearing nothing but a towel.

"Hi, Josie." She held up her hand, waving her long fingers one at a time. Frances towered over me, which made me feel even smaller than her presence alone. She was at least six feet tall and weighed no more than 130 pounds. He limbs were long and thin, but make no mistake, she was not weak. "Did you oversleep?" she asked, jutting her bottom lip out with feigned concern, her eyes wide. They were light, sparkling blue, almost white. That was a witch thing. Witches had bright colored eyes that looked as if they could pierce right through you. They were much more vivid than human's. "Poor thing," she smirked, then, took her long nails and ran them through my hair. I stepped back, so she pulled her hands back, calmly, and ran her hands through her short, blonde hair instead. It fell just above her shoulders. "If only you had set an alarm…" she trailed off as she turned to walk away from me slowly, almost begging me to follow her. It worked.

I followed closely behind. "Did you turn off my alarm?" I asked, suddenly furious. Frances had a problem with me since our first year together. My gut told me it was because my parents were two of the most well-respected witches in our world. Their powers were strong much like their parents and their parents' parents. My mother's side of the family was famously powerful. She was still spoken about to this day. That meant I had strength in my blood, and spells would come naturally to me. And they had. I was usually at the top of my class without much studying at all. Frances would die before she admitted it, but my hunch was she harbored a secret resentment for me.

"That is quite the accusation, Josie." She came to a sudden halt and spun on her heels to face me. "You know as well as I do it's against the rules to enter another student's room without permission. Especially to sabotage them." She raised her dark eyebrows as if she was daring me to continue but smirked at the same time letting me know she was proud of whatever she had done.

"It's also against the rules to use spells against other students," I pressed, refusing to back down. She might be nearly a foot taller than me, and there might be a part of me that actually was scared of her, but I could never let her see that. As soon as I did, she would pounce.

"What *exactly* are you implying?" she asked, flashing a brilliant white smile and looking down on me with her piercing eyes. Something in her not-so-innocent smile told me I was right. She had done some sort of spell to stop my alarm clock. It wouldn't have taken much, and she wouldn't have necessarily even needed to be in my room when she did it.

Since I had my answer, I didn't need to continue the conversation. There was nothing much I could do about it besides go to the Headmistress to have a formal complaint meeting. I *could* retaliate and sabotage her in some way. But then I would be breaking the rules, too. And Frances would run to the Headmistress the second it happened. She certainly wasn't above being a snitch if it benefitted her.

I brushed past her and made my way to the mirrors. I heard her giggle as I walked away, as if she enjoyed making me miserable. I looked down the long line of mirrors, scouting for an open one. The bathroom was shared by the whole floor. There were witches of all ages and grades on my floor so it could get pretty crowded in the mornings.

The mirrors were much too large. The black siding on them started at the green marble floor and stretched all the way to the ceiling. There were more than a dozen lining the wall, but only one was open. I rushed to claim it. I was between two girls I recognized from our frequent run-ins at the bathroom, but I had never actually spoken to them. I remembered them from their eyes though. That might be one of my favorite parts about being a witch, as shallow as it may sound. I loved looking at the different colors of my fellow classmates' eyes. The girl to my left, a third year, had deep blue eyes that looked like the ocean at night, but they still shimmered somehow. The girl on my left, a final year, had golden eyes that were so brilliant they were almost yellow.

I realized I had been staring too long when the final year gave me a side-eyed glance as if my gawking was intrusive. *Oops.* I mumbled a "sorry" and started unpacking my makeup. When I looked in the mirror for the first time, I groaned. My long, black hair was a complete rat's nest. I had obviously slept well. I took a second to look at my own eyes in the long mirror as I yanked my black brush through my hair. They were emerald green and glaring, with long, thick lashes lining the edges. My eyes were my favorite part about myself. I loved the way the color glowed. They reminded me of my mother's, and I could feel a sense of comfort wash over me every time I looked at them.

"Hey!" yelled a familiar high-pitched voice in my ear as two hands clamped down on my shoulders. "There you are!"

"Hi, Lillian." I was awake enough now to think rationally and wasn't annoyed with her anymore. My oversleeping was thanks to Frances, not my innocent best friend.

"I didn't want to wake you this morning. You were out cold," Lillian said, tip toeing to stand beside me in front of the mirror. If I had to choose one word to describe Lillian it would be "delicate." She was small, even shorter and thinner than I was. I stood at 5'3" and Lillian was nearly a head shorter than me. Her hair was bright red and styled into a pixie cut, although she was attempting to grow it out. It was past her ears now in an awkward in-between state. I still thought it looked cute— almost anything would look cute with Lillian's dainty features—but she felt self-conscious about it. In fact, as soon as she jumped in the mirror beside me, she began tugging on her hair, obviously displeased with how it looked. I hated to see her feeling anything but self-assured. So, I gently tapped her hands and pulled them down from her hair.

"You look cute," I reassured her. Her purple eyes softened, and she dropped her hands. A small smile spread across her red lips. Everything about Lillian was unique, down to the shoes she wore. She stood out from the crowd in a way that would make me jealous if I didn't so desperately desire to blend *into* the crowd. I looked at her smooth, pale skin through the mirror and smiled with pride. My best friend was really something special. "I *did* sleep well. Thanks to Frances," I informed her as I tossed water over my skin, rinsing my face wash off.

Lillian's thin, brown eyebrows raised, shocked and confused. "What...do...you...mean?" she asked slowly.

"She put some kind of spell on my alarm clock," I whispered, so no one could overhear any gossip. I had already decided I wasn't going to tattle. "Or maybe she used a sleep charm on me. I don't know. I sort of confronted her this morning."

"What did you say?" Lillian whispered, eyes still wide with surprise. "It's against the rules to do that! She can't use spells on her *classmates*."

"She was really the one who said something to me first, which tells me she is responsible no matter how innocent she acts." I rolled my eyes.

"What is her problem?" Lillian hissed. "Do you think we should tell the Headmistress?"

"Honestly, I just want to avoid the confrontation. Unless she does something worse than a sleep charm, I think I'll just handle it myself." I was almost finished getting ready. I applied one layer of mascara before shoving everything back in my bag. "Are you ready for class?" I asked. We had our first hour together, and she was already dressed in her burgundy skirt with black tights underneath. She had her black, silk shirt buttoned up to the top, so it was nearly a turtleneck, and tucked into her skirt. I hated our school uniforms, but Lillian always made them look cute. She even had on a small pair of black heels with studs decorating the top to complete the look.

"Yep!" she responded, eyeing me up and down. "I'll walk with you while you change, though. Let's go!" I glanced at the clock. We had 10 minutes to make it across campus.

Lillian grabbed my hand, I grabbed my bag, and we took off back down the long, dimly lit hallway and into our room. I unlocked our door as quickly as I could, running to my wardrobe beside my bed. Luckily, I had already ironed my clothes and hung them up. The high neck, black silk shirts were required for everyone, but we had a *tiny* amount of freedom when it came to our bottoms. Lucky us...

We could wear pants, shorts, skirts, or capris, as long as they were the same shade of burgundy the dress code required. I had my favorite pair of high-waisted pants picked out. I struggled to shove my legs in and almost fell over a couple of times, sending Lillian into hysterics. I finally got them on, tucked my shirt into them, and slid on my black ankle boots. I did a quick look in the mirror. I hadn't had time to style my hair. It was naturally wavy which meant on good days I didn't even need to curl it, but on bad days I looked like a tangled mess if I didn't. Luckily, today was a good day.

"Good enough," I shrugged. "We've got six minutes."

"We can make it!" We both took off down the hallway again, this time towards our classroom. We didn't run this time, but we were walking much faster than our fellow classmates. Several people turned to gawk. The stone halls were small, and we got stuck behind witches taking their precious time on our way. That slowed us down a bit, but as soon as there was a break in the crowd, we wiggled our way around them. Scurrying down the main spiral stairwell, we finally made it to the garden. Almost in the clear.

The air was cool as we stepped outside and I shivered. October on the island was chilly, but somehow still green. As we walked through the garden, I noticed most of the flowers were out of bloom, but the trees and bushes were still dark green. I glanced at my watch. "It's 7:12," I breathed a sigh of relief. "We're going to be two whole minutes early!" Slowing our steps, we began to walk a normal pace and catch our breath. We continued down the dirt path to the classroom doors on the other side.

When we reached the classroom, it was mostly full. People usually arrived 10 minutes early to this class since they knew how important being on time was to Professor Rose. I made my way to my assigned seat in the back while Lillian made her way to the front. We were in alphabetical order, which meant we never got to sit together at assemblies or in classes where professors actually still assigned seats. I was always towards the back since I was a Parker, and Lillian was at the front since she was a Bishop.

We sat at tables of two, so we had a partner to work with when we practiced charms. My tablemate was already seated with his book out. I only saw the back of Miles' head as I walked towards my seat, but my heart was fluttering. I didn't know how I got lucky enough to have a last name close to "Preston," but I thanked the Divinity I had *him* as my partner.

As soon as I sat down at our table, a smile spread across Miles' face. His white teeth stood out against his dark skin making his smile even more breathtaking than I would have thought was possible. When he smiled, it wasn't just with his mouth. It lit up his whole face, including his green eyes, which were just a shade darker than mine today. His eyes were one thing I always looked forward to on these mornings. They alternated between blue and green, so I never knew which shade to expect.

"Hey, Josie," he greeted me.

"Hi, Miles," I smiled back, feeling a hint of pink touch my cheeks. I couldn't help but blush whenever he acknowledged me. Pathetic, I know. I had been obsessed with Miles all of last year despite the fact that we had barely spoken when we sat together at assemblies. But this year we had two classes together and became friends. I actually thought we were a little flirty now, but that was probably all in my head. Most of the girls in our grade thought he was gorgeous, so I knew it would be a far stretch to think he was interested in me.

Last year was Miles' first year at the school. I still didn't know how he got away with not coming to the school for the first few required years. I was too scared to ask. If his parents were hitches, then he wasn't here because he wanted to be. And who knows what would have happened to his parents in that case.

"How are you this morning? Cutting it a little close," he teased.

"Yeah, I know. I overslept," I said, rolling my eyes at myself. He didn't need to hear the Frances drama. I admired his deep blue, velvet blazer. That blue was the required color for 5th year students. Miles was technically old enough to be a 5th year, but he was still in several 4th year classes since he came to school late.

Just then Professor Rose appeared at the front of the classroom. It was impossible to tell how old she was in human years since witches all aged differently, but I'm sure the number was high. Small wrinkles were beginning to develop around her eyes and her hair was a shade of grey. Even witches eventually started aging. It just took a little longer than it did in the human world. Despite her age, she was still gorgeous. The way she carried herself was elegant, and I had never seen her look anything less than glamorous. She floated down the rows as she addressed the class.

"Good morning students," she smiled. Her voice sounded like velvet. I watched the way she moved and hoped I would age as effortlessly as she had. Even though she was a strict professor, I admired her. And everyone respected her. That is probably why they gave her the most interesting class to teach: "The History of Witchcraft." We learned about the origin of spells and covens. We even covered the witch trials that occurred around the world and how the leaders of covens had to work hard to keep our kind a secret. The way she taught it was captivating.

"Good morning, Professor Rose," the class responded in unison. She continued floating through the rows as she reviewed our lesson from last week. Her dress was tight and light pink hitting just below the knees. She had on a white blazer with shoulder pads, which may have looked outdated on most people, but not her. Her heels were incredibly high, but she breezed past my desk with ease. Her lashes were so long and full I thought they surely must be fake. She was stunning, but that didn't distract anyone from her brilliance or kind heart.

The class was an hour and a half, but it always passed quickly. Partially because it was so interesting, but also because even when the material wasn't captivating, Miles was. I found myself peeking at him out of the corner of my eye from time to time. I had carefully developed a technique to admire him undetected. I propped my head on my left hand and leaned forward slightly, letting my hair fall over my face. Then, through the spaces in my hair, I peeked at his face. It sounds creepy, sure, but I honestly could not help myself. I started today's admiration at the bottom of his face. He had smooth skin with a strong jawline, but it was still gentle somehow. I was in the middle of admiring the curve on his bottom lip when I saw his eyes on me, as well. *Crap!* I was caught. Red-handed. I slowly turned my eyes back to the front of the room, but before I did, I could swear I saw him wink. My face was blood red now, so I kept my hand glued to my face in an attempt to hide the shade. I didn't dare look at him for the rest of the class.

As soon as Professor Rose wrote our homework on the board and dismissed us, I scooped up my books and started to walk out of the room to meet Lillian. Before I turned to leave Miles stopped me. "Josie, can I ask you something?" *Oh no. He thinks I'm a freak. Please don't call me out for staring. Please. Please. Please.*

"Sure," I responded with a voice three octaves higher than my usual pitch. *Keep it casual.* If he did call me out, I could say he had something on his mouth. Food. Leftover food from breakfast. That is why I was staring directly at his lips. That seemed believable enough.

"Are you free tonight?" he asked, his smile as brilliant as ever. *What...did he...just ask?*

"Uh, y-yeah," I stuttered, still shocked by the question, and dropped my books on the table a little too loudly. Why were my legs suddenly numb? I put my hands on my hips then let them fall at my side, then put them back on my hips again, unsure of what to do with them. This was officially embarrassing. *Oh, get it together!*

"Would you want to do something? Just the two of us?" By this time students were filing out of the classroom so I knew Lillian would be waiting for me and watching our interaction. I prayed she couldn't overhear the conversation. I was already nervous enough and my pink cheeks were giving that away to anyone who walked by. She would be grilling me after class.

"Yeah. That sounds fun," I replied keeping my voice calm. "What do you want to do?"

"I've got something in mind. Can I meet you at your room around 8:30?" he asked with a slight smirk.

"Sure." The less I said the better. If I started rambling, I would embarrass myself even further.

"Cool. It's a date. I'll see you then." He slung his bag over his shoulder and walked out of the room. I made sure he was gone before I let my jaw drop. When I regained feeling in my legs, I turned around to find Lillian standing right behind me. I could tell by her face that she had heard everything.

"Holy Divinity! Josie!" she squealed. Professor Rose, who was still at her desk gathering papers, turned to look at us. "Sorry, Professor Rose. We're leaving now," Lillian apologized. Professor Rose smiled slightly, and I hoped she hadn't heard my conversation, too.

The chilly air rushed across my face, cooling my hot cheeks. It felt nice and cleared my head a little. "Is this real life right now?" I whispered, partially to myself and partially to Lillian.

"*How* are you so calm? You've been crushing on him all year! I'm freaking out more than you!" Lillian exclaimed too loudly. The garden was filled with students traveling from class to class. Heads turned in our direction.

"Lillian, lower your voice!" I whispered yelled. "Believe me, I am freaking out, but I can't go around campus screaming 'hip hip hooray.' I have to remain poised."

We made it back to the main lobby of the school with the large spiral staircase. We didn't have the same class for the next hour, so we walked here together every day before splitting up.

Before Lillian headed in the opposite direction, she

grabbed my arm. "You are going to give me every detail later."

I just nodded. "See you later, Mrs. Preston."

"Shhh!" I turned to go in the opposite direction as quickly as possible, with the biggest smile planted on my face.

2
FIREFLIES

My room was a disaster when Lillian tiptoed in, bouncing around piles of clothes and mismatched shoes that were spread across the room. She was so agile she reminded me of a ballerina. I had been in the room for an hour, searching for something to wear tonight. I knew it didn't *really* matter what I wore. I'm sure Miles didn't ask me out because of clothing, but he had only ever seen me in a school uniform. I wanted to feel confident. At least that's what I told myself. If I was being honest, I just needed the distraction. If I thought about tonight too much, my stomach felt uneasy. Focusing on clothes was much easier.

I ran out of room on my bed and started tossing reject items onto Lillian's bed. She didn't even attempt to move anything. She just sat on one of our roommates' beds instead.

It was already 8:00, and I hadn't been able to talk Lillian about the upcoming date. We had lunch together like usual, but we were never the only people at our table. She knew better than to bring it up in front of a crowd. I told Lillian pretty much everything, but she was the exception. I was a private person otherwise.

I found it difficult to trust people. I wasn't sure where the trait came from since my parents were the exact opposite. They trusted everyone and didn't have a shy bone in their bodies. I always admired them: the way they could walk into a room and make conversation with anyone there; the way our dining room had constantly been filled with people, witches and humans alike, over for dinner parties. That was so far from the person I was, and sometimes I hated that. I wanted to be more like them. I wanted to be more like my mother, who would have had no problem walking into this date with her head held high and hours' worth of conversation ready to go. But that wasn't who I was, no matter how hard I tried to force myself to be open. Lillian knew that better than anyone. So, she knew asking about a date would not be a casual lunch conversation for me.

"You can borrow something of mine if you want," Lillian offered, and I felt so thankful to have her. Anxiety was written all over my face, and even though I knew she was dying to know the details, the first thing she did was try to help me. I dropped the white blouse that was in my hands and trampled over the pile of clothes to hug her, feeling instant relief when her tiny arms wrapped around my waist. "Are you really *that* nervous?" she giggled, dropping her arms.

"I am really nervous, but I'm also glad I have you for a best friend. You're basically the only person I can trust." She smiled with pride. I knew she felt the same way about our friendship. "But your clothes are way too small for me. Thank you for offering though. I'll just have to find something in this mess," I spun around gesturing to all the clothes thrown around the room, "because I've cleared out my whole closet." I wasn't even exaggerating. My closet was bare except for one pair of old, navy heels that I only kept for special occasions and a grey sweater dress, which was far more itchy than cute. I should probably just throw it out.

I didn't have an abundance of clothes, and I wished that Lillian and I *were* the same size. She had so many clothes that she had to keep some of them in *my* drawers. Plus, she was naturally stylish. I wasn't completely clueless, but I hadn't been shopping in years. Not since the last time my mom took me. So, my wardrobe was small to say the least.

"There is plenty here that we can work with," Lillian said, standing up to look through the clothes. She only had to rifle through three piles before she had an outfit for me. "Here. This will look cute!" She tossed the dress to me, and I slipped it on. I turned to look in the mirror beside Lillian's bed and found she was right. It didn't look half bad. It was so simple I would have never considered wearing it. It was a plain white, loose-fitting dress that fell just above my ankles. "One more thing," she said, tossing her blue jean jacket towards me. I slid it on. It was about two sizes too big for Lillian, so it actually fit me. With my black ankle boots, the look was complete.

"Well?" I asked, giving a twirl.

"You look perfetto!" Lillian cheered in a terrible Italian accent. She had been practicing the language recently.

I rolled my eyes and laughed. "You may need to work on that before you spend First Semester Break with your family in Italy."

I only had fifteen minutes before Miles would arrive, so I started picking up the disaster area. With Lillian's help everything was back to its usual place in under 10 minutes, which was good because there was a knock on the door at 8:25. I was already anxiety-ridden, so the knock startled me, and I jumped.

"He's early," Lillian whispered. "Someone's excited," she added, eyeing the door. "Good luck." She smiled, grabbed a book, and sat down casually on her bed. I made my way to the door and took a deep breath before opening it.

"Hey, Josie," Miles breathed when the door was open. He seemed a little nervous, too, which made me feel more comfortable, oddly enough. Overly confident people always make me extra tense.

"Hi," I said in return. I looked down and noticed he had flowers in his hand. Five tulips perfectly in bloom.

"These are for you." I grabbed the flowers, hesitantly, thinking of how bare the garden was this time of year. There were basically no flowers in sight.

"Thank you! But…how…?"

"A simple charm does the trick. I've been doing some studying outside of my classes on how to alter the elements of nature. They should stay in bloom for a while, too."

"Thank you," I mumbled again, walking over to my dresser to set them down. Lillian grabbed them before I could.

"I'll find a vase for them," she offered. "That was very thoughtful, Miles," she said, glancing in the hallway.

I walked back over to the doorway. "You ready?" I asked and he nodded in response. I stepped into the hall, closing the door behind me, and walked slightly behind him, letting him take the lead since I had no idea what the plan for tonight was. There were only so many things you could do on this tiny island. "So, do I get to know where we're going, yet?"

"I think you'll find out rather quickly." We walked through the winding halls of the castle, talking about easy topics, like school and our friends. Despite my nerves, I felt comfortable talking to him. Miles was so warm and kind. He was the type of person I felt like I could be myself around without worrying about being judged. I sensed that about him the first time we actually spoke. He joked around with me the very first day of Professor Rose's class. So open. It reminded me of how my parents treated everyone. Maybe that's why I liked him from the start.

We walked out the front door of the school and began crossing the bridge that led outside school grounds. It was my favorite type of night. The moon was just barely there in the sky and the stars were bright. The castle stayed mostly dark at night, so it was easy to see the stars if you wanted to. There were no other buildings or any roads at all on the island.

We continued across the stone bridge slowly as it took us over the moat surrounding the school. There were streetlamps lining the bridge, but they were dimmed quite a bit. It was very foggy, which wasn't out of the ordinary. The island stayed covered in fog a majority of the time. To the right was the ocean. If we were just a little closer, I would be able to hear the waves crashing. To the left was the forest, called the Black Forest. The fog covered the ground and the trees shot high in the air. A chill went down my spine as I remembered my nightmare from last night.

"Are you cold?" Miles asked, already slipping off his jacket.

"Oh no," I shook my head and pulled at my jean jacket. "This is cozy. It's just a little spooky out here." I didn't need to go into detail about my freaky dreams on the first date.

"Here," he held out his arm and I wrapped my own around it while my heart doubled its pace. "I'll keep you safe," he smiled down at me.

When we reached the end of the bridge, I thought of how much this looked like a scene from a horror film. For a normal human it would be a scary thing, but horror films were my favorite. It was probably a witch thing. Nights like this usually brought me comfort. When they didn't remind me of terrifying nightmares...

We reached the end of the bridge and I stopped, letting go of his arm. "Are we getting close? We're about to go off school grounds, you know?"

He turned back to look at me. "That rule doesn't really apply to me. I have connections." He winked and continued walking. I followed and didn't ask what he meant by that. I wasn't the type to break rules and neither were my friends. In fact, I had never been off school grounds without a professor. But, to my surprise, I didn't even feel nervous. I felt excited.

We turned to the left, heading towards the woods. "Are we going to the Black Forest?" I asked and my voice quivered a little, but not from fear. The temperature was dropping as we got closer to the forest. I could see my breath.

"Are you cold or are you scared?" Miles asked, looking down at me with his green eyes.

"Just cold," I assured him. He took his arm and wrapped it around me, pulling me closer to him. I warmed instantly, but it was mostly from the heat rushing to my cheeks. My heart fluttered, and I snaked my arm around his waist to let him know I approved of his move. We were walking on a dirt path now, and I looked over my shoulder to watch the school fading into the distance. In front of me, the only thing I could see besides the trees was the guard shack twenty feet ahead. It was a small room with white siding. There was a single lamp on inside the room and a dim light on the roof so you could see it from far away.

"Are we going to sneak past the guard?" I whispered shocked, but slightly thrilled.

"We won't have to." We were approaching the building and Miles didn't break his stride once. He strutted up to the front door confidently and knocked. An older man stood up from a chair on the side of the room to open the door. His hair was grey, and he moved across the small room slowly. I wondered how many years he had been on this Earth. Miles greeted the man as I stayed a few feet behind them.

"Good evening, Mr. Dan." Miles held out his hand and shook Mr. Dan's hand firmly. He was talking a little louder than usual, so I figured Mr. Dan was hard of hearing.

"Hello Miles." The man looked happy to see him. "I haven't seen you in a couple weeks. Where've you been?"

"I've been busy with school. I haven't been able to make it out much." What was Miles doing in the Black Forest?

"Well, how is your uncle doing?" asked Mr. Dan.

"He's doing much better," Miles responded, keeping his answer short as if he didn't wish to elaborate.

"I see you have a guest tonight," Mr. Dan said, gesturing towards where I stood in the shadows.

"Yes," Miles replied, walking towards me. He looped his arm around me again and led me towards the light shining from the top of the building so Mr. Dan could see who he was meeting. "This is Josie. I thought I would show her some of the tricks I've been practicing out here."

"Well, you two have fun," he said cheerfully, waving goodbye and wobbling back into the guard shack. I heard the radio click on, playing swing music quietly, before we walked away from the shack towards the Black Forest.

I had never been out here at night. The chilly air and fog reminded me of All Hallows Eve, our most celebrated holiday, which was coming up in a couple of weeks. "Being out here at night makes me feel festive," I whispered as we took our first step into the tree line. I took one last look at the school. It glowed softly and beautifully at night from the torches surrounding it. "Next week they'll be putting up the decorations."

"Why are you whispering?" Miles giggled as he whispered

like I had.

"I don't know," I laughed, still whispering. "I guess I feel like we're breaking the rules being out here alone. At night."

"Well, technically, we are."

"So, you come here often, then? Out in the Black Forest? Alone?" I asked Miles, curious and slightly teasing since it did seem a little creepy he spent evenings here. "The guard seemed to know you very well."

"I come out at night sometimes to practice spells involving nature. I came to the school late, as you know, so I feel like I need to work even harder to catch up. Plus, nature spells are the most intriguing to me. It makes me feel a connection to the earth. I could show you one if you like." He stopped, unraveling his arm from my waist.

"What kind of spell exactly?" I questioned timidly.

"Don't worry. I think you'll like it." He turned away from me and began whispering a spell I couldn't make out. It was dark in the forest. The skyscraper trees formed a canopy of sorts, blocking out most of the sky, but a few streams of light from the stars trickled down. It was silent with the exception of crickets, a few owls, and Miles' whispers. Then, all of a sudden, it wasn't. The chirps of crickets and calls of owls and ribbets of frogs grew louder. The area in front of us was suddenly illuminated by a thousand tiny glows. It looked like Christmas lights covering every inch of the air. I turned to look behind me and found that the lights went all the way around us in a circle. They were fireflies. And they took my breath away as they reminded me of the lights that used to cover my house on All Hallows Eve. Only this light was brighter. All Hallows Eve celebrated the dark side of witchcraft, so the decorations often represented that. But this magic wasn't dark. It was light. My favorite type of magic.

I exhaled a "wow" and smiled, feeling at peace. Miles whispering slowed and the light began to fade, until it disappeared altogether along with his whispers. He turned to face me again, smiling. "What'd you think?"

"It was...beautiful. I didn't know a spell like that existed," I said, still mesmerized.

"They don't really teach magic like that in school. I've just learned it through my personal studies. The first time I tried it—Well, all the white light...it reminded me of you. A bright light in a dark place." He looked at the ground as he said the last line like he was too shy to admit it. My heart fluttered. He thought of *me*?

"I don't know if you could give me a better compliment than that," I glowed. Instantly, I felt sure of his feelings for me. I had been dreaming of him ever since the beginning of the year. And when we started talking in class, I would have never imagined he would develop feelings for me. He was better than me in every way—confident, kind, smart, and nothing short of gorgeous. I could see the way girls ogled him, hear how they spoke about him. But he thought of *me*.

Bravery washed over me for a short moment, and I decided to take advantage of it. I took four steps, closing the distance between us. Facing Miles, I slipped my hands in his. Then rose to my tiptoes slowly so our lips were inches apart. I paused, waiting for him to close the distance between us this time. He leaned forward a bit but paused to look in my eyes. His looked softer than usual. I fluttered mine closed as he pressed his lips to mine. His hands released mine and moved to my face. He gently cupped my cheeks as our lips moved together. My head swam. This was even better than I imagined it would be. He pulled his lips away first but pressed his forehead to mine. His hands were still on my face, but he moved his thumb to trace my bottom lip. My heart was beating so hard I was sure he would hear it. This wasn't my first kiss, but it was the first that ever meant anything to me. The first that made me feel something.

Miles moved away and grabbed my hand. "Come on." We continued into the forest. It should have only been half a mile long, but once you were inside the woods, whatever magic was here seemed to make it extend endlessly. We didn't say anything. I was too busy focusing on deeply breathing to lower my heart rate. As I wondered if he was doing the same, we reached a small opening in the trees. Miles grabbed a small blanket out of the bag he had been wearing on his back and laid it on the ground. "Have a seat," he said, motioning towards the blanket. I obeyed and sat down. Miles grabbed three logs from a pile a few feet away from us and stacked them onto one another. He whispered "ignis" and small sparks started popping up from the logs until they were on fire.

"Very impressive," I said looking at him and raising my eyebrows.

"Yeah, I'm kind of a big deal," he teased. He sat down beside me on the blanket and we both faced the fire. "So, tell me more about your life before this school. I know Josie here at North End, but how about who you are outside of the castle? Where are you from?"

"Well, I'm mostly from a small town in West Virginia, but I lived in a couple different places when I was really young. I mostly remember West Virginia though, so I guess that's what I consider "home." We moved to Scotland the year before I came to North End. What about you?"

"I never really know how to answer that. I moved around a lot. Like *a lot*. So, nowhere has ever felt like home. I grew up all over the United States, though, and me and my dad eventually moved to Italy when I was a teenager. Until I came here."

"Wow. Very interesting. I've never been to Italy," I commented.

"It's beautiful, but I was glad to move here, honestly."

"What took you so long? To come to this school, I mean. Usually people start when they're thirteen," I asked, silently praying that the question didn't lead to a story about his father being locked away or killed for keeping him from this place.

"Uhm…it's a complicated story. But basically, my dad…turned his back on the witch world." He glanced over at me cautiously, probably wondering if he should continue or if I was already judging him. His dad was a hitch. And most witches didn't like to associate with those types of people.

He must have seen on my face that I was unbothered by that fact and continued. "My mother and him split up a long time ago, and she pretty much left me behind. I haven't talked to her since I was seven or so. After that, my dad didn't want anything to do with witchcraft. Maybe it reminded him of my mom, I don't know, but we moved around a lot after he stopped practicing magic. Probably to keep witches from finding us, but I didn't know that at the time. Anyway, he tried to keep me away from this world, too. He wasn't open about my powers, even when he must have known they were developing. I didn't understand for a while. But when I did, I started researching and reaching out to family I hadn't spoken to in years. Eventually, I found out about North End and enrolled myself as soon as I could. My uncle, my dad's brother, helped me with it all."

"How did your dad feel about that? Is he still not practicing?"

"He was…accepting. I think it made him sad, especially since I was moving away, but he has his own life. And yeah, he still doesn't practice magic. His powers have faded a lot over the years, so I'm not sure he could even if he wanted to."

"Didn't the school…punish him when they found out he didn't send you here?" I asked bluntly, even though I was still afraid of the answer.

"No, they didn't," Miles shook his head. "My uncle is very high up on the council at the school so when all of this came out it was a mess. He knew his brother was keeping me a secret, but he never turned us in. So, when I reached out to my uncle, he had to tell them the truth: that he had a nephew who he knew had been hiding. They couldn't punish my father without punishing my uncle, and they would never punish a witch as high in the ranks as my uncle. The council is very loyal to their own, perhaps to a fault."

"So, he got lucky?" I asked. Miles was being polite when he described the council as "loyal." Rumors always led me to believe the council was corrupt. It all depended on who you knew. And if you knew the right people, you could get away with anything.

"He got *very* lucky. So did I," Miles exhaled, shaking his head. "I was a little angry with him for keeping me from this world, but I couldn't imagine losing him. He doesn't deserve to be killed for choosing to live a different way, even if he didn't handle the situation perfectly. No one is perfect. Not even parents." His last comment made me think of my father, and I wondered if it made him think of the mother that abandoned him years ago. We sat in silence for a moment while I processed what his childhood had been like. It was obviously very different from mine and coming to this school must have flipped everything upside down.

"Well, are you happy with your decision?" I asked, finally breaking the silence.

"Yes," he said without hesitation. "Very. I would have resented him if I didn't at least try the school. And now that I'm here, I'm really happy. I finally feel like I belong."

"Well, I, for one, am glad you ended up here." I bumped him lightly with my shoulder in an attempt to lighten the mood.

"Me, too," he said with a smile on his face, bumping me back with his shoulder. "Hey, maybe don't mention much about my dad around school. If other students hear he's a hitch..." he stared into the distance for a moment choosing his next words carefully. "I just don't want anyone to say bad things about him. Plus, my family has done some other things that a lot of people here wouldn't approve of. Things far worse than letting magic fade..." Miles' voice trailed off and his expression looked hard, closed off. So, I didn't press the issue any further.

"Anyway, what about you? I know you came to school here as soon as you could. So, I assume your parents are still faithful witches?" My heart sank a little. If you were raised in the witching world then you knew the story of my parents. But Miles hadn't been. I hated telling people the sad parts of my story, but I wanted Miles to truly *know* me. And this was a piece of me. So, I took a deep breath and began.

"They were both very powerful witches. My mom was in line to be Headmistress of this school actually. And my father used to work high in the ranks of our coven. Everyone knew how powerful they were, especially my mother, but they were so modest. They never let the power go to their head like some witches do. They were open and kind." Once I got started telling someone all the good things about my parents, it was difficult to stop. I could have rambled on for ages. "But…uhm…a few years ago my parents were in an accident. We lost Mom." I paused to swallow the lump forming in my throat. "Ever since then my dad…he hasn't been the same. He was there when it happened. He tried to save my mom, but he couldn't. He had to witness losing her firsthand. And his mind suffered. He stays in our home in Scotland now. I see him sometimes, but he never leaves the house."

"Geez. I'm so sorry, Josie. I had no idea," Miles said. He

put his arm over my shoulder, and I leaned my head against his.

"It's okay," I lied. "One day I can tell you more about them. Maybe even break out the old home videos. I love showing people how vivacious they used to be. They were really special."

"I don't doubt that. If they created you, they must have been extraordinary, Josie." I felt him gently press his lips to my hair. "So, if they were *that* powerful, you must be very gifted." I could hear the smile in his voice.

I pulled my head back off his shoulder and laughed. "I don't know if I'd say that."

"Don't downplay your powers, Josie. I have a class with you. I've seen a little. And I've heard things around school," he said, winking at me.

"What in the Underworld have you heard?" I asked, my eyes widened, mortified. Being the center of any sort of gossip was one of my worst nightmares.

"Nothing bad at all. Just that you would go far in this world. Your parents must have been well known, too, because people seem to realize you have a natural gift. Plus, you are the most gorgeous girl at this school. That alone makes you stand out more than you might realize."

I scoffed. "That cannot be true. I'm glad *you* think I'm cute, though." I smiled and looked away, suddenly overwhelmed by my nerves.

"I didn't say 'cute.' That would be a disservice. I said 'gorgeous.' You stand out of the crowd. And not just your looks. The way you carry yourself, the way you treat people. You're a good person." My heart fluttered. "I've wanted to ask you out for a while. I've tried to hide it. My efforts may have been in vain. Maybe you've known that for weeks." I looked back at him to see he was the one blushing now.

"I felt the same about you, but I'm sure *everyone* could see that. I can't hide anything. My face gives me away every time." I pointed to my brilliant red cheeks.

"I hoped you did." His eyes burned through mine again, and it felt as though the forest moved around me. Was he casting a spell or was this just the effect he had on me? I didn't have much time to decide before his lips were on mine again and I wasn't able to concentrate on anything, but the way they felt moving with mine.

We spent more time in the Black Forrest talking, kissing, and laughing, before we began the trek back to the school. We had no idea what time it was, and neither of us had wanted to move from our magical spot beneath the trees. But the second time the fire died down, we knew we needed to get back before our roommates started worrying.

Miles walked into the guard shack to say goodnight to Mr. Dan before we left, and I waved from the outside. Mr. Dan's face lit up when he saw Miles, and I watched as he handed him something. Mr. Dan waved at me from inside the booth as Miles exited and took my hand.

"Mr. Dan wanted us to have these." Miles held out his other hand. There was a small white handkerchief concealing something. I took it hesitantly and unraveled it to find two chocolate chip cookies inside.

"My favorite!" I giggled. I grabbed one and immediately took a bite. Mr. Dan seemed so sweet and it suddenly seemed so strange that I had been at this school all these years and never even knew he existed. I wondered how many other genuine people worked in the castle that I had never crossed paths with. It gave me hope. Even though dark magic lurked here, there was just as much good.

The lights in the school were dimmed more than before and some halls were pitch black. It was well past curfew. We walked slowly and silently, listening for any professors who may have still been awake. We knew how easily we could be caught, and it made my heart pound. As we walked through a dark hall, I lit a small light using a spell and held it in my hands. It illuminated a path for us. When we reached my bedroom door, Miles gave me a kiss on the cheek before turning to walk to his room.

I opened my door expecting Lillian to be up waiting for me, but the room was black. The only light was the moon shining through the window. I closed the door behind me, making as little noise as possible. I changed into my pajamas silently, but when I went to crawl in bed the springs beneath my mattress creaked, giving me away. Lillian sat up straight in her bed. I felt badly about waking her, but I was relieved at the same time. I was dying to tell her all about the night. She crawled out of her bed and joined me on mine and for the next hour that is exactly what I did.

3
WEEKLY CONSULTATIONS

I woke up on time this morning, which was a blessing and a curse. I stayed up much too late last night talking to Lillian about my date and only got four hours of sleep. It was worth it, though. Luckily, today was Friday, which was my easiest day of classes. I only had one in the morning, then my weekly meeting with Professor Howard.

Another rule of the school is that we have to meet with our mentor for an hour each week. My mentor was Professor Howard. Our meetings reminded me of the therapy I attended for a year after my mom died. It was my dad's idea that I joined him in therapy, and he insisted we both go twice a week, once separately and once together. I think it helped me, but it didn't do anything for my dad. He was desperate to feel better, desperate to be there for me, but nothing could fix him. He was too broken. He started sharing less and less each week until he didn't speak at all. So, I made the choice to stop going. My dad didn't have that choice. Soon after the accident he was hospitalized for not taking care of himself and my coven ordered him to attend. As far as I knew he still went every week, though I couldn't imagine him doing anything besides sitting on that couch in silence.

My meetings with Professor Howard reminded me of that. We could talk about anything during the meetings: School, magic, friends, family. It's basically just a check in. Honestly, Lillian and I theorized that it's a way to keep tabs on young witches, to make sure they don't go rogue. There's been a history of young witches getting together and trying to overthrow headmistresses. In one case, two witches even attempted to do dark magic in the human world. It didn't work out well for them. The weekly meetings seemed like an extra step to try to stop things like that before they got too far.

If that really was why we were required to attend, then it was pointless for them to waste time interviewing me each week. I had no desire to take over anything. I didn't even want to move up too high in the ranks of North End's council. I knew others expected that of me, though, since my parents were so high up at our school. But all of that didn't fit my personality. I just wasn't born a leader. And I was completely fine with that.

Thankfully, I had time to have my usual breakfast this morning. I went to the café and grabbed a blueberry muffin and an apple juice before heading to the balcony. The café was quiet. It was still a bit early for most students to be eating. A majority of them just ran in and ran out 10 minutes before class, scarfing down their food on the way. Only four other students sat in the café and two on either side of the balcony. I sat alone at a table in the middle and looked out at the view while I ate. The sun was rising, painting the grass an auburn color and the ocean a silver. I brought a book with me, so I studied in between bites and glances at the landscape.

I was able to take my time getting ready as well, which was nice because I needed time to mentally prepare for my only class of the day. Though I only had one class on Friday, it was my most difficult for a couple of reasons. First, it was intense subject matter. The spells we learned in this class were not cute charms like I was used to. They were dark spells. Ones that could harm others. The school claimed they taught them in the name of self-defense, but it still made me uncomfortable to have the spells in my mind, to study them at all.

This class required focus. You couldn't relax for even a moment because if you did someone could get hurt. It was draining. Especially since the material was challenging for a 4th year to learn. It was a 5th year level class, but the Headmistress allowed the top four witches in their class to take it a year early.

Which led to the next reason this class was so difficult. One of the other 4th years in the class was Frances, who, in my opinion, seemed a little *too* excited to be learning about dark magic.

When I entered the classroom, I saw her sitting in the front row. This class was taught by the Headmistress herself, and she didn't believe in assigned seats. She said free seating made it easier to see which of us were truly eager to learn and which were not. Naturally, Frances was never late to *this* class. She arrived even earlier than me and plopped herself front row and center. *Suck up.*

I made my way to the fourth row and sat down, opening up the same book I brought to breakfast to review my notes from last week. I honestly didn't need to study *too* often for my other classes, but this one was different. One simple mistake could injure someone...or worse. So, I was extra cautious.

I reviewed the material from last week for 10 minutes or so as students filled the seats around me. I didn't have friends in this class. I didn't know many of the 5th years, and even if I did, I probably wouldn't spend much time talking to them during this hour. There was a creak at the back of the room and several heads turned to stare in that direction.

The Headmistress, entering through the same door as we had, made her way down the middle aisle to the front of the class. As she moved forward, her heels clicking on the marble floor, the chatter in the classroom died down until it was silent.

No one spoke while the Headmistress taught unless they were asked a question that required direct answer. It seemed that every student in the school was frightened of her. Even some of the professors seemed nervous when she was around.

No one could blame them for being scared. The Headmistress wasn't an average witch. You only received this job if you were overly qualified and one of the most powerful, well-versed witches of all covens. Headmistress Craw had already held this job for two decades. She was going to step down a few years ago, so my mother could take her place, but it never got to that point. She was in the accident before she could take the title of Headmistress.

My mother would have been a very different leader than Headmistress Craw. She was *good*. She basically exuded a white light. She was powerful, yes, but certainly not scary or dark. So, the exact opposite of Craw. Craw is one of the oldest witches I've ever come across, which is likely why she was going to step down a few years back. The rumors suggested she didn't necessarily *love* the idea of moving on from her position, but she trusted my mother and knew her time to retire had come. Craw welcomed her with open arms and put her own feelings aside for the good of the school.

Craw was fair in that way, but she was also stern and loved her power, perhaps a little too much. Her high heels clicked down the aisle until she came to a stop at her desk, located directly in front of Frances.

Craw wore a deep red dress. It was long-sleeved and practically plastered onto her body, hugging every curve. Black tights covered her legs. Her makeup was extravagant, and anyone could guess it was because she longed to be youthful again. She always covered as much of her body as she could. If she didn't, it would be impossible to look past her age. No one knew her exact age, but it was rumored she was nearly 200 years old. Her skin had begun to sag and wrinkle intensely. It was a greyish color, as well, but she hid that with as much makeup as she could coat on her face. Her hands were the only part that showed what her skin truly looked like, and she typically wore gloves to cover that. But today she didn't have them on so I couldn't help but fixate on their strange color.

The room was so quiet you could hear a pin drop. Craw's eyes slowly moved from side to side, scanning the room. They were foggy, but you could tell they used to be bright, clear silver. I used to wonder if the fogginess affected how well she could see, but I now guessed her vision was clearer than any of ours.

Once she scanned the room several times, she parted her red lips to speak. "Good morning, my students," she cooed. Her voice still surprised me sometimes. Based on her appearance one would expect her voice to be deep and stern. But it was the exact opposite. It was rather high pitched, light, and delicate.

Craw began her lesson by reviewing the dark magic we learned last week. It was a spell that would leave our opponent paralyzed, stunning them. If there was enough power behind the words and they were repeated enough, it would permanently paralyze the victim. We practiced on insects, not people, but that was enough to make me uncomfortable. I hated thinking of how terrified the creature in front of me must feel when I took away its ability to move. It was alarming when we went over it last week, and I felt a wave of horror wash over me as she reviewed it now. The idea that another witch could deprive you of the use of your limbs by simply saying "opstupefacio" was one of the most dreadful things I could imagine.

She spoke of real life examples of the spell that she witnessed herself. Craw was a proud Follower of the Fallen Angel, and she spoke of him often in our class. Only his Followers—the Followers who have actually done his bidding—would have witnessed this spell in action. Followers of the Divinity or even Followers of the Fallen Angel who worshiped from afar would never use such a spell.

"*I* have never used this on a human subject," she claimed, "but I have seen it used by someone else. It is not something to perform casually. However, when the Fallen Angel calls on you, you must do as he says. His wishes must be obeyed." She smiled when she said his name and it sent chills down my spine. The Fallen Angel didn't call on his ordinary Followers. It was said that he only called on witches who sought out the work on their own accord, witches who had truly dark intentions. Craw claimed she no longer sought out his work and only worshipped him from afar, but she used to work closely with him. I didn't want to imagine what terrible spells she'd cast in her life.

There were also rumors around school that Craw had been a mistress of the Fallen Angel, and that was how she landed this job in the first place. People said she sold what was left of her soul to him, giving herself to him completely in exchange for power. This was a terrifying thought even though I didn't know how true it was.

"So, as you all know from last week's lesson, this spell will momentarily paralyze your victim. Today, we will discuss how you can not only paralyze the *body* of the victim, but also the internal organs and bodily functions, such as the heartbeat, permanently. In order to do so, you must have more than one witch say the spell. Does anyone know how many witches it would require to complete such a task?"

I knew the answer. I had read ahead in the text as I studied this morning, but I was in no rush to answer. I wasn't a fan of having all eyes on me. But seconds ticked by and no one raised their hand, so I slowly put mine in the air.

"Ms. Parker?" Headmistress Craw called on me. Several eyes turned to look at me, including the pair belonging to Frances.

"It would require at least three witches to complete that task, Headmistress," I answered, timidly.

"Very good. Thank you, Ms. Parker." Headmistress Craw began circulating the room, continuing with the lesson. All the eyes turned away from me and back to the Headmistress except Frances'. I peeked at her from the corner of my eye. She was so furious her tan face had turned a shade of red. I giggled to myself, suddenly glad I had chosen to share the answer with the class.

The lesson continued and I took notes diligently, not missing a single syllable. Some of the stories about the victims of this spell made my heart hurt, and it was difficult to write the words, but I did so anyway. I supposed I needed to know this information in case I needed to protect myself one day. Just the thought made the hair on my arms stand up. The class ended at exactly 9:15 a.m., as usual.

I closed my book and stood up, smoothing my maroon skirt out before putting my book in my bag. When I looked back up, Francis appeared out of nowhere. She was hovering above me, her judgmental eyes piercing through mine. She sneered as she said, "Clever answer in class today, Josie."

I rolled my eyes before brushing past her to head out the

door. She made a show of jerking her shoulders back as if a stampede had hit her. "Excuse you," she scoffed and grabbed my arm, spinning me around to face her. "You owe me an apology."

"What is your problem, Frances? Seriously. What have I *ever* done to you?" I questioned, pulling my arm out of her hand. I was feeling more confident than usual. It probably stemmed back to my incredible date last night. I was still on cloud nine. Frances seemed a little startled by my response, but quickly covered her shock with anger.

"Oh, don't act so innocent. You have a problem with me, too, little Miss Perfect. You're jealous of me." She raised her eyebrows and smirked. "It drives you mad that the Headmistress *loves* me and barely speaks to you."

"The only thing that bothers me is that you suck up to her. If I really thought you wanted to work hard and learn I would respect you," I spat back. "This is the only class you even bother to show up on time to. Seems fake. Like you care more about appearances when someone 'important' is around."

"Hmmm...see...I don't think that's it. I think you're angry because I might be more powerful than you." She took another step towards me and stared down. "You're not the only one in this school who is gifted, you know. And I intend to show everyone what I'm capable of."

"I never said I was gifted, Frances." I saw the

Headmistress staring at us with a stern look on her face and decided it was time to leave. "Have a good day." I turned and walked away. This time she didn't try to stop me. She must have noticed the Headmistress looking at us, too. Before the door closed, I heard her say, "Headmistress, could I ask you a quick question?" Her voice was coated in sugary sweetness.

* * *

"So, are you going to tell me what's bothering you?" Professor Howard asked. He was seated in front of his large oak desk that he had stained coal black. He leaned back in his leather desk chair casually, refusing to break eye contact. His sapphire eyes honed in on mine until I looked away. I was still angry about the confrontation with Frances, but I didn't know what complaining to Professor Howard would do besides make me seem immature. I didn't want that. I distracted myself by looking at the arrangement of his desk.

Professor Howard was very neat. It was obvious he liked things to look a particular way and any stray from his path wouldn't be well received. He had a notepad directly in front of him. Sometimes he would take notes on our meetings. He usually only did that if I mentioned my parents, though. I guessed it was so our conversations were well-documented in case I ever expressed dangerous thoughts, like hurting myself or others, since it wasn't completely out of the ordinary for a young witch to take a turn for the worse and use their powers for something less than productive. Plus, a young witch going through a traumatic event, like losing their mother suddenly, might ring a few warning bells to some. Not that *I* would ever hurt anyone.

I never expressed such feelings. I never went into detail about what happened with my parents either. I only mentioned them when I talked about my childhood and discovering my powers. I knew Professor Howard wanted to know more or felt like he should at least ask because he often did, but I never budged. It wouldn't be a pleasant discussion.

Professor Howard's desk had silver trays on it. Trays that were filled with files, each labeled with identical white tags in the left-hand corner with the same perfect handwriting. The files had names of places, classes, and spells on them. A few of them even had the names of students on them. These students were on his caseload, which meant he met with them for consultations, too. That led me to my next reason for being less than willing to talk about my squabble with Frances. She was on his caseload. I knew he would never mention anything to her about our conversation if we *did* happen to talk about her. That was against the rules. But it still felt weird.

"Is it school?" he probed. "Are your grades suffering?" I shook my head, but still refused to make eye contact as I continued scanning the desk. He kept three small sculptures of the Fallen Angel front and center. They were black and had the same character in different poses. The character was broad with muscles covering every part of the body. It looked very similar to human form, but still resembled no human I had ever seen. The character didn't wear any clothing. Two horns protruded from its forehead. The figure showed off a set of sharp teeth by curling back its lips. It looked very similar to pictures I saw of the Fallen Angel in textbooks, but the figures on Professor Howard's desk sent a chill down my spine every time I saw them. There was something sinister about seeing the figure free from the confides of textbook pages.

I looked away quickly as Professor Howard asked his next question. "Is it your father? Friends, perhaps?" He did *not* want to let this go. My eyes wandered to the wall behind his head. It was covered in diplomas with the name Wilmot Howard and awards of various sorts, which wasn't out of the ordinary. If you were a professor here, you had to be brilliant. And if you aged as slowly as witches did, you had plenty of time to learn.

"Josie." His voice was stern this time. I forced myself to make eye contact with the man sitting in front of me. Professor Howard was very good-looking. All of the people I sat with at lunch dubbed him the "hottest professor" last year. When I looked at him objectively, I couldn't help but agree. He was a bit older, but not ancient. I could tell his age had been frozen for a while, but he still held on to his youth. However, the way he carried himself was very distinguished and mature. He sat up straight always, with his broad shoulders facing me. His features were sharp, and his hair was black with streaks of grey, always styled perfectly with some sort of gel. Light grey scruff lined his chin, but he never let it get long enough to form a full beard. Today he wore dark blue jeans with black dress shoes on his feet, and a tan, chunky sweater. Yes, he was objectively handsome, but he didn't appeal to me the way he did to other students. To be *that* attracted to a professor felt very, very wrong.

"I'm fine," I insisted.

"I know that look," he said, leaning forward and pointing his pen at me. My heart pittered. Could he tell I was thinking about how good-looking he was? He finally smiled. "Okay, okay. We don't have to talk about whatever it is." *Phew.* I knew he would drop it after that. He respected boundaries and could tell he was crossing mine. "So, what *do* you want to talk about, Ms. Parker?"

I shrugged my shoulders. "I don't know, Professor. Honestly, meeting every single week seems excessive to me. We always run out of things to discuss."

"And I always let you leave early. So, we don't waste time, really," he countered. He was right. If we ran out of things to say and he couldn't pry anything else out of me, I was always dismissed. "I think it's good to have the time set aside in the event you *do* have something you wish to talk about." Curiosity struck me. How old was Professor Howard? He spoke as if he was from a different time, but when? Would it be rude to ask? Witch ages remained somewhat of a mystery to me.

"Could I ask *you* a question?"

"Mhmm," he responded simply, folding his hands across his stomach.

"How old are you?" I asked, hesitantly. He raised his brows and smiled slightly as if my question surprised him. Which it likely did. We didn't talk about *him* much. He took a deep breath and sighed. He was silent for a full minute. I heard the large, antique clock above the door to his office clicking. I started to wonder if he was going to answer or if I should redact my question.

"Well," he began, "I suppose you're asking in terms of human years." I nodded. "I was born in 1935. So, that would make me 85." The words didn't match the man sitting in front of me. This man looked no older than his late 30's, but he had been on this earth for 85 years.

"How does it work? Aging as a witch?" I asked. Since he was willing to tell me that much, perhaps he would be willing to answer my other questions.

"It is a complicated thing. Even I have a difficult time wrapping my head around it. There is no sound answer that can be backed up with evidence, but many say it has to do with your genes, much like it does for humans. If you come from a strong, healthy line of witches then you tend to live longer. Unless fate intervenes." His eyes flickered to mine when he said, "fate intervenes." Like it had for my mother. "It isn't unheard of for witches to live to be 300 years old, but that seems to be a rarity. I have also heard darker rumors. In old legends, there was talk of witches selling their soul or stealing those of others. The witches that sold their soul to the Fallen Angel lived to be several hundred years old, but they usually lost any semblance of good they had in their hearts. Their years were typically spent doing the bidding of the Fallen Angel. And the tasks were never pleasant. The Fallen Angel doesn't show mercy, even when mercy should be shown."

I was taken aback by his last comment. It seemed like he was speaking negatively of the Fallen Angel—something Followers are forbidden to do. "What types of tasks did they have to do?"

He sighed deeply and I could see he was reluctant to go into detail. "Murder, kidnapping, torture. You name it. The tasks almost always did harm to others. Dark magic. I am not sure how one could justify these deeds are worth the extra years if the years aren't truly yours to live."

"What are the other rumors you've heard? Besides soul selling? How do you...steal a soul?" I pondered. This was the most explanation of aging I had ever gotten from a professor. Plus, the less we talked about me, the better.

He laughed. "You are too young to be worrying about your mortality, Ms. Parker. Let's move on. This subject is quite grim." We spent the next 15 minutes discussing my classes casually. The conversation wasn't enthralling so my mind continued to wander back to our discussion on age. Witches had sold their soul to the devil in order to live longer. Free will seems like a high price to pay for an extended life when we already lived longer than average. He also mentioned stealing souls but avoided my question about it. If Professor Howard was reluctant to tell me the stories, then they must be very dark. He had no problem telling me about the consequences of selling your soul to the devil. What could be worse than that?

Our session ended early. The full time wasn't necessary. I grabbed my bag from beside the chair and stood up. Professor Howard walked me to the door and wished me well. When I opened the door I almost ran straight into a tall, slender body: Frances.

She looked down at me and smiled. "Hello, Josie," she cooed with faux friendliness. She was acting sweet in front of Professor Howard. Frances was one of the many students who had a crush on him. I'd overheard her saying some crude things about him in the past.

"Hello," I said curtly. I didn't care to put on some sort of a show in front of Professor Howard. "What are you doing here?" I asked, suddenly paranoid she had been outside of Professor Howard's office eavesdropping this entire time.

"Well, it's time for my weekly meeting, of course. What else would I be doing here?" She smiled, showing all her teeth and winked at me. Professor Howard was standing right beside me. There was no way he missed that. I wondered if all the young female attention made him uncomfortable.

"I thought our meeting wasn't for another hour," Professor Howard questioned, crossing his arms across his chest.

"I was hoping we could push it up a bit. I just have *so* much to talk to you about," Frances said. Her voice was honey.

"Come on in, then, Frances. Ms. Parker, I'll see you next week." I stepped out into the hallway and Professor Howard disappeared into his office. Frances turned around to close the door, and when she did, she looked me right in the eyes and licked her lips.

4
THE FIRST VICTIM

"I thought I would go with a more traditional date than our first. No special charms in the Black Forest," Miles said while gazing down at me. That same gentle smile was painted on his face and his icy blue eyes were sparkling. *Blue today*, I smiled as I admired the color.

"What does that mean exactly?" I asked. We were walking down the hallway hand in hand. I was surprised by how normal this already felt. Safe. I could hear echoes of laughter and cheering down the halls. It was 9:00 p.m. on a Friday evening, which meant parties were in full effect. Our parties were a little different than in the mortal world. Witches weren't big on drinking unless it was a special occasion. Alcohol was banned from the campus anyway, so it was a rarity to have a student sneak it in. Instead, students spent weekends staying up late, performing charms and spells, playing pranks on each other, or staying up all night with their friends. Sometimes a few kids would organize magic competitions, but mums the word on that. The administration had no idea. A few of the bold students drank experimental potions from time to time, but I had never tried that. Normally I would have been in one of my girlfriend's rooms with Lillian trying to see who could stay up the latest, but I didn't mind my company tonight.

"I thought we could rent a movie from the library and watch it in my room, if that sounds okay to you," he said, almost like a question, to make sure I was comfortable with the idea of being alone with him in his room. Spending time in a boy's room wasn't a normal activity for me. It was also frowned upon by some professors; not necessarily against the rules as long as you didn't stay past 11:00 p.m., but if the wrong professor saw you, they would do their best to embarrass you.

"That sounds fun!" I replied with a little too much excitement. I was going for enthusiasm, but I was worried it came off more hysterical. I was completely comfortable going to Miles' room, but the idea also turned my stomach into a ball of nerves. I could feel it twisting. "What kind of movies do you like?" I questioned, forcing myself to sound nonchalant.

"I'm cool with anything. I'm pretty easy to please when it comes to movies. If it's funny, I'm all in. What about you?"

"I'm the same way. I love horror films and comedies. The

only kind I'm not a fan of are sad movies."

"Why don't you like sad ones? Do they make you cry?" he asked seriously. He sounded genuinely curious.

"Yeah. It's really easy to make my cry, though. If a dog dies in a movie, my week is ruined. I just don't understand why someone would want to watch a depressing movie. If you want to be sad, you can just walk outside and live your life. Plenty of sad things happen every day," I explained. A few years ago, I wouldn't have cared if we watched a sad movie. Movies that focused on loss and pain didn't used to hurt me the way they do now...because before I had never experienced real loss. True pain. Now sad movies just brought back the memories of my parents that I tried my best to block out.

"That's true." He said it like he understood what I was referring to but didn't press for more details. I appreciated that. "How about we watch a comedy, then? We both enjoy those." He slipped his hand out of mine and wrapped it around my shoulder in a comforting way. The conversations we had last time were probably etched in his mind. He knew the tragedy I had seen. His arm around me was a small gesture, but it made me feel less alone in that moment.

"Sure," I smiled. We continued walking until we reached the west corridor. Miles opened a small, red door on the right side of the hallway and had to duck so he wouldn't hit his head. The door led us down a slender staircase. So slender that we couldn't walk beside each other. So, Miles walked ahead of me. We were heading to the library through a back way. Not many people used this staircase and I wondered why he had chosen it. There were only two small lights on the walls, which made it difficult to see where we were going. I was starting to regret coming this way at all when we came to a window with no glass separating us from the outside world. Just a hole cut out of the stone. Miles stopped when he reached it.

"Come look," he said. I could already feel the cool breeze blowing through the stairwell. I looked up towards where we just came from and saw an endless number of stairs until they disappeared into the black. I bent down so I could stare out the window. The breeze brushed my face and I inhaled deeply, taking in the smell of the ocean. I could see the tall grass blowing in the wind below us, the ocean in the distance, and the sky decorated with one million points of light. We stared in silence at the view. "Beautiful, isn't it?"

"Yes," I said breathlessly. "There are good things in this life, too."

He turned his head just enough to press his lips against mine for a moment before whispering, "Yes, there are." His blue eyes blazed through me for a moment.

We began our descent again, wordlessly. We reached our exit quickly after that. But before we opened the door, I looked down and saw the staircase continued spiraling into darkness.

"I wonder what's down there…" I said.

"I don't know, but I don't want to find out," Miles replied.

He pulled me through the exit of the stairwell, and I could see the library up ahead. The ceilings were very high in this hallway with shiny mosaic tile decorating the ceiling. The walls were wide leaving ample room for people to walk. Not that we needed it. Not many people were walking to the library on a Friday night. We approached the large, black arch that opened into the library. I had never spent much time here since my room and classes were basically on the opposite side of the school. If I ever needed to study, I just used the textbooks from class and reviewed the material on the balcony in the early mornings. I hadn't explored much outside of what I learned in my classes, but Miles had, and it was obvious right away.

When I walked past the arch, my eyes wandered everywhere. There was so much space. The ceilings were the highest I had ever seen. They shot all the way up exposing four levels. Each level expanded. I wasn't able to see how far from where I was standing, but every floor was lined with bookshelves. I wouldn't even be able to guess how many books were in here. The walls were all white and the floor was made up of colorful tiles. It reminded me of a historic church I visited in Scotland once.

While I was awestruck, Miles wasted no time grabbing my hand and leading me in the right direction, which was a relief because I could get lost on my own. We made our way towards the back of the library, passing large wooden tables that were scattered around the room. Each was adorned with their own antique lamp that allowed students to study late into the night. I only saw three other students on our way to the very back. The library had more light than the hallways, and I quickly realized that part of the reason for this was the glass ceiling. I looked up and could see the million points of light again, as well as a bright sliver of a moon.

We trekked through well over half of the library, and as we were closing in on a section most students avoided—the dark magic section—I began to get nervous. But Miles suddenly took a left turn, veering away from the dreaded section. We walked between two tall bookcases to a room encased with glass. Inside were more rows of cases, but instead of books lining their shelves there were hundreds of DVDs. To the outside world I assumed DVDs were outdated, but North End didn't even have cable, so this was high tech for us. Technology wasn't very important in our culture. Most witches associated it with the human world, so they either had no interest or need. But even witches enjoyed watching films from time to time.

Miles pushed open the glass door and stretched his arms out as if he was presenting the room to me. "Here we are! Comedies are right over here." I followed him to the comedy

NORTH END: THE BLACK FOREST

section.

"You must spend a lot of time here. You know your way around," I commented as we browsed the selection.

He simply shrugged. "I like to read. You pick one movie and I'll pick another. Then we'll decide between the two." I liked the way he had things planned out already, instead of putting me on the spot. I wasn't great with decision making. We didn't spend much time browsing. I picked out one option and Miles did, too. He held them behind his back and told me to pick a hand.

"Hmmmm. Left?" I said as I pointed towards his left hand. He held out the movie that I had picked. "Yes!" I cheered, even though I didn't care what movie we watched. I barely even remembered the title.

* * *

When we reached Miles' door, he hopped in front of me to unlock it and hold it open. "After you," he said. I stepped in. It wasn't the first boy's room I had ever been in, but it was by far the nicest. I wondered if his uncle had hooked him up with a nicer room. It was on a corner which meant more space. And instead of one large window he had two, but they were both covered with tall, black curtains identical to the ones over my window.

"Can you see the ocean from here?" I asked, pointing toward the window.

"Not quite, but you can see the Black Forest, which is kind of spooky at night." He pulled back the curtains, and I cupped my hands on the glass so I could see outside. There it was. The Black Forest in all its spine-chilling glory. The fog was, of course, covering the ground below the trees. It was straight out of a horror film.

"Nice," I said, awkwardly. I pulled back from the window and turned to face Miles, suddenly realizing he was standing very close to me. Our bodies were almost touching. Neither of us said a word, but I could practically feel the electricity in the air. Suddenly, I wasn't sure what to do with my body. There was only one chair in the room, and it was under a desk on the other side of two beds. I shifted my weight to my right foot and crossed my arms not wanting to assume I could just plop down on his bed. Luckily, Miles took the lead by taking a step around me to sit down on his bed first.

"Have a seat," he told me as he patted his bed. "I'll get the movie set up." I took a seat and leaned back on his pillows trying to look relaxed.

"My roommates are at a party so it should just be us for a while," he said as he put in the DVD. I didn't even have a DVD player in my room. It must have been his father's. He was part of the human world after all.

"Do you like your roommates?" I asked, glancing over to their side of the room. It was littered with clothes and old socks. Miles' side was the exact opposite. Neat and tidy.

"Yeah. They're good guys. We're not best friends or anything. Probably because I keep to myself a lot of the time, but we get along. How about you?"

"Well, my relationship with Ava and Daliah is like the relationship you have with your roommates. They're fun to be around and we've grown close this school year, but we aren't *best* friends. Lillian is my third roommate, but we're more like sisters."

"Yeah, I don't think I've ever seen you two apart during lunch," he laughed.

"We've been best friends since my first day here. I was scared and shy, hiding in the corner and she came over to me."

"She seems really sweet. We should all hang out sometime. I've never really talked to her."

"She'd like that. She's heard all about you," I slipped. My cheeks burned with embarrassment, but Miles turned to look at me with a grin on his face.

"Really?" he asked. I just shrugged and pretended to admire his posters of different famous landmarks around the world so I didn't have to make eye contact. Miles had the DVD set up and came to join me on the bed. He laid back on his pillows, too. His bed was full size, so we weren't forced to squish together, but our bodies were still tilted slightly towards each other, our hands just an inch apart. I still felt the electricity in the air and a magnetic pull to touch him. I was glad he left the lights on.

The movie started to load and previews for old films popped up on the screen. "Josie," Miles whispered, his voice rough. I turned my head and his eyes were burning through mine. "I--I," he said like he was searching for the right words to say. Then his lips were on mine. This kiss wasn't like the rest. The spark was palpable. We moved towards each other, and I wrapped my arms around his shoulders. My legs intertwined with his. I pulled back to take a breath and inhaled his cologne, some sort of spice, and his breath—minty. Before I could think again, he pulled me back in. I wasn't sure how long we stayed like that—our bodies interlaced, his hands moving down mine. All of a sudden, the theme music for the music began to play. Loud. It startled me and I pulled back, jumping.

We both laughed and I said "sorry" breathlessly. He leaned in to give me one more kiss on the cheek before turning to face the TV. He kept one arm around me though. I laid my head on his chest and finally relaxed. I could feel his heartbeat under my head, slow and steady. Every so often he would run his hands through my hair or kiss the top of my head, and his heart rate would quicken just a little. I couldn't focus much on the movie. I was too busy soaking in this feeling. With Miles, I felt almost complete. I hadn't even come close to feeling this way since I lost my mom.

I was so happy when I was growing up. I never questioned if I was loved or felt like something was missing. Then Headmistress Craw and Professor Rose showed up at my room that night, and everything I knew came crashing down around me. They told me about the crash, how my father tried to save her. As soon as the words came out of their mouths, I felt a hole rip through my chest. Something in me was gone. I felt the sharp pain of that hole every minute of every day until this moment. The hole was still there. It always would be, but the pain was dulled. Lillian helped with that, too. I knew I was never completely alone. She was my family. Now Miles felt like part of that, too.

I kept half watching the movie and cuddling Miles for a while until he wiggled out from under me. "Care if we pause this for a second? I need to run to the restroom."

"Sure," I said. He pressed pause and mumbled a "be right back" before heading out the door. It was somewhat quiet, but I could hear mumbles of students in other rooms. Not sure what else to do, I started looking around. There were posters hung on every wall. His roommates' posters mostly consisted of cars and bands. I glanced behind me to see Miles had a painting of the Colosseum in Italy. I wondered if he bought it while he was there with his dad.

Miles still wasn't back, so I looked at the books he had sitting on his nightstand. A couple were classroom textbooks I recognized, but a few must have been from the library. A book of charms. A book about nature. At the very bottom was a black book with a textured cover bound by a leather strap. There was no name on the binding of the book. I didn't want Miles to come in and see me looking through his books like a snoop, so I turned back to lay on the pillows again. A few minutes passed by and there was still no sign of him. Curiosity started to get the best of me. I had never seen anything like this book before.

I got up and sprinted to the door, looking both ways down the long hall. It was empty. Miles wasn't headed back yet. *One peek wouldn't hurt*, I told myself. I went back to the nightstand and picked up the book. I felt a pang of guilt now that it was in my hands. *What if this is his private journal?* If that was the case, I promised myself I would close it right away.

I undid the leather band and noticed there was no name on the front cover either. Just rough, black material. I opened to the middle of the book to find a page of spells handwritten in deep red ink. But I had never seen them before. I wondered how advanced Miles was in his practice of witchcraft. He obviously studied a lot more than I did, but I couldn't be *that* far behind him. Were these his personal spells he was attempting to create? That would be very advanced for such a young witch.

I flipped through the book slowly, not because I was looking too intently at the spells, but because the pages were so thin and fragile it seemed like they might fall out of the book or disintegrate, even. I reached the final page in the book and finally found a title of some sort. In bold print, in the middle of the page read "Angelus Mortis." My hands began to tremble.

A scream pierced through the walls and echoed through the halls. It was a loud, shrill shriek of mortal terror. I yelped in response and tossed the book back on the nightstand before jumping onto Miles' bed. I sat for a moment, listening, but only heard silence. Then the footsteps of more than one person shuffling in the hall. I slid the black book underneath the rest, right where I found it and stood. It sounded like the footsteps were heading towards where the scream came from, so I ran to open the door.

Several boys were lingering in the hallway by their doors while a brave few were making their way to the end of it. That was where the scream came from. I moved timidly out of the door frame and, pausing after each step, made my way towards the end of the hall. My heart sputtered with anticipation and dread. I could see it before I got too close. The horrified looks on the boys' faces. The terror on the two girls who seemed out of place in the hallway filled with boys. Their hands were covering their mouths and their eyes were wide.

There on the floor at the end of the hallway where the paths branched in three different directions was a girl, who looked even younger than me, crumpled on the floor. The way her body was arranged showed that more than a couple of her bones were broken. A pool of blood was coming from her head. It was too much to look at. I went to turn away and go back to the room, but at that exact moment Miles came around the corner with blood soaking his shirt. His face was emotionless.

I froze. "Angelus Mortis" means "angel of death." Just then the Headmistress came storming around the corner with three of the medical ward staff behind her. She turned to the crowd of people gathered in the hall.

"Get back to your rooms immediately!" Her voice was ice and her cloudy eyes were wild with alarm. The medical staff picked up the body of the young girl and moved her to a gurney. The crowd started moving quickly around me. They knew better than to wait around for the Headmistress to ask again. But I was stuck. My eyes were locked with Miles'. His mouth dropped open like he was in shock. I wanted to cross the scene and ask him what was going on, but the Headmistress said, "Preston, come with me." She grabbed him firmly by the arm and led him down the hall.

"I'm sorry, Josie," he said before he turned his head and

disappeared around the corner. The body of the young girl was being wheeled down the hall behind them. I was alone in the hallway then and I started to shiver harder and harder until I was nearly convulsing and couldn't stop my body from moving. What should I do now? Why did Miles say he was sorry? I didn't know exactly what happened to the young girl, but her surviving seemed impossible. If another witch was responsible for her injuries, should I be walking the halls alone? I decided to go back to Miles' room even though the empty, silent walls didn't sound appealing. At least I could safely call Lillian from there and ask her to come walk me back.

Without being fully aware of the motions I was going through, I made it back to the room and sat on the bed. My shaking had slowed, but I felt like I was going into some sort of shock. My pulse had quickened, but it was returning to normal now and an unwelcome numbness was spreading over my body. I pulled my flip phone out of my pocket and dialed Lillian. My voice was too calm on the phone and it confused her.

"Wait, wait, *what* happened?" she asked. "Guys, shut up! I can't hear Josie!" she yelled to the group of girls that were laughing in the background. I heard a few giggles and one girl say, "Tell her to kiss her boyfriend for us!" It sounded like my roommate Ava.

"I think someone died," I repeated softly. "A girl was

found in the hallway here. Miles is gone and I don't know what to do." My voice was even and suddenly I was so thankful for the numbness. If I thought about the situation for too long, I would surely go into hysterics.

"What happened to her?" Lillian asked with terror in her voice.

"I think she was murdered," I stated as calmly as if I were discussing a school assignment.

"We're coming to get you," she responded firmly. "Give us five minutes." The phone went dead and I sat in silence waiting for them to come. Any noise from gatherings or parties I was able to hear before was now gone. It was so quiet I could hear my ears ringing. Laying back on the bed, I pictured everyone in their rooms, sitting with friends or alone like me, and staring at the walls, trying to understand what just happened, what we just saw. Some of them had probably never seen a dead body before. I had only seen one.

Maybe some were whispering theories about who did this to the girl. I refused to let my thoughts go any further than that. If I started wondering who had done this, I would start thinking of the black book on Miles' nightstand, how he said he was sorry, and the expression on his face when he rounded the corner with blood on his shirt.

The door swung open without a knock and Lillian barged in. Our roommates, Ava and Daliah, followed her. "There's blood on the floor out there, Josie! What happened?" Lillian whisper-yelled.

"I'll tell you everything I know when we get to the room. I can't stay here anymore," I replied, nearly jumping off the bed. She nodded and put her delicate arm around me. We made the walk back to my room in silence. On our way, an announcement was made over the intercom. Headmistress Craw ordered each student to return to their rooms and lock the doors. She said there had been an incident and a student was attacked, but she didn't divulge anymore. She didn't need to. Word traveled fast in this school. The students with phones had undoubtedly already texted their friends, and the ones that didn't would meet in the bathroom to exchange information tonight.

Our pace was swift as we made our way to the room. Down our hall we could hear doors lock and sealing spells mumbled. When we got to our room, we did the same, joining hands and repeating "signati Ianua mali spiritus" three times to seal the door.

"There. That should do it," I said feeling reassured. "No one outside of this room can come in without us lifting the spell first." We spent the next couple hours talking about what had happened tonight, with the exception of the book on Miles' nightstand. I wasn't ready to explain that yet. I did tell them about the scream, the shocked faces in the hallway, the girl on the floor, and finally the blood on Miles' shirt. I was quiet after mentioning that last detail.

"You don't think he *killed* her, do you?" Ava piped up. She was horrified, but I could see in her eyes she was enjoying this just a little. She loved gossip.

"Josie, I'm sure he found the girl first and tried to help her. He was probably the one that went to get Craw," Lillian comforted me. We were both sitting on my bed and she had her tiny arm wrapped around my shoulder again.

"Yeah, Miles is a really good guy. I've talked to him a few times in the library. He would never hurt anyone," Daliah said. But her words didn't make me feel much better. Talking to someone a few times doesn't mean you know who they are. Even I didn't know Miles *that* well. You can't really know who anyone is behind closed doors.

Even with that being said, I still didn't feel like he would be capable of hurting anyone. I remembered how I felt lying in his arms. He made me feel safe and comforted. I went to the Black Forest with him *alone*. If he was going to harm anyone, why wouldn't he have done it that night? I realized all of their wide eyes were still focused on me, waiting for me to say something.

"I know," I finally responded. "I just need to talk to him, and I'll feel better. I can't imagine what he's going through right now. If he was the one that found her...he must be terrified." I pictured Miles walking down the hall and seeing the girl; maybe picking her up in his arms, unsure of what to do. I shook my head to clear the thought.

"I bet he'll call you tonight once he's finished meeting with Headmistress Craw," Lillian said. I hoped she was right. The other girls started theorizing about what happened to the girl and whether she survived or not. I suddenly hated that we were all referring to her as "the girl." None of us even knew her name, yet here we were gossiping about her and the sinister people who might be in her life. I kept my mouth shut while they spoke of hopes of her recovering because I knew after what I saw in the hallway she couldn't possibly have survived. If she had, she would never be the same. She would be traumatized. Like my dad.

Ava thought the girl was attacked by her boyfriend. She went on to explain her made-up idea. The girlfriend had cheated. The boyfriend found out and killed her in a fit of rage. Another idea that was floating around through text messages was that there was a serial killer on campus. Which made no sense to me since there had only been one murder, but that small detail didn't stop Ava from forwarding the idea to all her friends. I guess it helped people to talk through upsetting things. Trying to rationalize made it feel less scary, like it was just a mystery movie we were trying to solve before the very end.

"Maybe another witch did it. Like they wanted her soul or something. To live longer," Lillian suggested grimly.

"What do you mean live longer?" I questioned, flashing back to what Professor Howard said in his office today. "Soul stealing," he had said with no further explanation. It felt like a lifetime ago now.

"My mom told me a story once about an old witch. She was very powerful. One of the most powerful in our history, and she was a devout Follower of the Fallen Angel. Her name was Mary Langley," Lillian began.

"I've heard that name before! She's written some of the spells in our textbooks," Ava interrupted, giddy now. I rolled my eyes. The last thing I felt was excitement.

"You're right, Ava. This started in the 1400's. Mary was one of the most powerful witches back then, so she came up with a lot of new spells that had never been done before," Lillian explained. The 1400's had been a renaissance of sorts for witches, since during the 1300's many witches lived in the mortal world. Some of them were exposed to plagues since they lived so closely with humans. There was no spell to combat disease at the time and even witches can die from things like that. It wiped out hundreds of our kind. Covens disappeared completely. Magic was lost because humans found spell books that belonged to those who died. The books were all burned out of fear. Some humans tried to hunt witches after this discovery, but they could never catch them, of course. They would have been overpowered easily. Many witches went into hiding and started keeping their distance from the mortal world while they rebuilt. Friends, families, and decades of spells were lost. Most covens learned their lesson and stayed away from humans after that, but, of course, some covens had forgotten the stories or didn't heed their warnings. This led to the witch trials in the 1600's. Even though those weren't nearly as devastating as what we had already suffered, they ended any relationships witches had with humans. Witches realized things could never change and mixing too closely with the human world, revealing all our secrets to them, only led to devastation for both sides. Even the few human friends my parents had were kept in the dark. They had no idea what we were.

After the plague in the 1300's covens tried their best to rebuild. Mary Langley was a big part of that. "Some of her spells were good," Lillian continued. "Like you said, we learn them here at school. But some of them were sinister. They caused witches to turn on each other. They were the darkest magic. Mary craved power and she would do anything to get it. When she started to age and grow weaker, she decided a century and a half wasn't long enough. Some say she created a new spell, some say the Fallen Angel himself gave her one of his own, but either way this spell would make her more powerful and keep her younger even longer. She killed a witch using the spell. And when she did, she syphoned the witch's soul, making her more powerful and youthful. No one knows how many witches she actually killed, but eventually she had to be taken out by her coven. It was clear she wasn't going to stop killing. She wanted to be as powerful as the Fallen Angel so she could work by his side, rule the Underworld hand in hand with him. Maybe someone else at this school knows that story, too. And they want more power." She paused after that and it was silent for a moment.

"That's seriously dark," Daliah said, but I was intrigued. I needed to know more about Mary Langley because there was no doubt Lillian's story just scratched the surface.

"Probably too dark. I'm not sure who at this school would even be capable of killing for that reason." The girls continued talking, but I suddenly felt exhausted. I laid my head on my pillow and started to drift to sleep listening to them chatter. I was honestly grateful that they were awake. Hearing their voices made me feel at ease. I finally fell asleep wondering what the young girl's name was.

5

A SUSPECT

My dreams were filled with darkness that night. I saw Mary Langley dressed in a hooded cloak. Her face was barely visible. I could see each step she took in the Black Forest, though I wasn't actually there. It was as if I was looking at everything from above, floating in the sky. Other dark figures that I couldn't quite make out followed her as she walked through the forest. The figures, whatever creatures or demons they may be, eventually stopped near a circle in a clearing. In the middle of the circle was the body of the young girl, crumpled on the forest ground the same way it had been in the hallway. Mary stepped into the circle and bent down placing her face on the young girl's. It looked like she was kissing her neck, but I eventually realized she wasn't. She was drinking her blood. When she looked up to the sky her eyes were crimson red.

That image woke me, and I let out a yelp as my eyes adjusted to the darkness. My breath was coming in quick spurts as I checked my surroundings. I recognized the features of my room: my bed, my blankets, my roommates asleep next to me. I was no longer in the Black Forest. My breathing slowed until it was back to normal. Lillian was in my bed, too. She looked up with her eyes still half closed. "You okay?" she asked groggily. I wasn't sure she was actually awake. Her red hair was going in every direction and I'm pretty sure she had drool on her face.

"I'm fine. Go back to sleep," I whispered. She didn't hesitate. She was out again in a matter of seconds. I rolled over and saw my phone was plugged into the charger. Lillian must have done that to make sure I didn't miss any calls from Miles. I snatched it up quickly. It was 7:45 a.m. and I had two missed calls from Miles. Relief flooded my body. I needed to talk to him. I slid out of bed and walked to the corner of the room as I dialed his number.

"Hello?" he answered on the second ring. His voice sounded tired, deep and hoarse, but tense at the same time.

"Hey. Were you asleep?" I asked, feeling guilty that I had woken him after what must have been an unbearable night.

"No. I don't think I fell asleep at all last night. I was really worried about you," his voice was gentle now.

"I'm sorry. I would have called, but I figured you would reach out when you were back in your room," I apologized. Sleep had given me a new perspective and I felt like I was looking at the situation with the proper view now. The new day cleared my vision and I was certain Miles could never hurt someone. Of course not. It was silly to doubt him for even a second.

"It's okay. The guys next door said your friends came to pick you up. Thank the Divinity they did. It made me sick to leave you in my room all alone after...what happened." That was what his "sorry" had been for; leaving me unprotected in his room. "But Headmistress Craw was not taking 'no' for an answer." He whispered as he spoke and I assumed his roommates, like mine, were still slumbering. I pictured him in his room with the lights off, snuggled under his covers, and wanted nothing more than to be there with him wrapped in his arms again. "I need to see you," he breathed, his voice desperate.

My chest flooded with too many emotions: longing for Miles, sadness for the girl, fear of the unknown. A sob escaped from my throat and suddenly I was crying, unable to stop the tears from slipping out.

"Are you okay?" he asked urgently. "What's wrong?"

"I just..." My voice came out all scratchy. I paused to take a few deep breaths and compose myself, fighting against the lump in my throat. I won and the tears slowed. "I think the shock is finally wearing off. I need to see you, too." I thought of how safe I would feel with my head on his chest and his arms cradling me. I needed that feeling.

I heard him breathe a sigh of relief on the other side of the phone. "I thought you might never want to speak to me again after last night..." his voice trailed off and silence followed. Neither of us wanted to discuss this any further over the phone. "I'm coming to get you. I'll explain everything."

"I don't think we're supposed to leave our rooms..." I whispered half-heartedly, but I desperately wanted to say, "to the Underworld with the rules." I hadn't felt safe since we'd been apart.

"Headmistress Craw is going to make an announcement this morning. They're still going to serve breakfast and after that she's calling everyone to the auditorium to explain what's going on. In detail."

"Do you want to meet in the café, then?" I asked, thinking of the long walk he would have to make just to come to my room first.

"No!" he almost yelled. He quickly started whispering again. "I'm coming to get you. We'll walk there together."

"Okay," I paused and listened to his breathing for a moment. "Miles?"

"Yeah?"

"Do you think something bad is going to happen again?" I couldn't bring myself to say the word "murder" out loud.

"I don't know, Josie, but let's not take any chances. I'll keep you safe no matter what." I heard the sincerity in his voice and something in my heart told me I could trust him as much as I trusted Lillian. "I'm on my way."

"I'll be waiting."

"I'll knock three times." He hung up the phone before I could respond. I knew I was a mess. My curls were knotted from sleeping and my eyes were puffy from crying, but that didn't matter. After last night, my appearance didn't seem so important.

I paced the room, tip toeing so I wouldn't wake anyone. I wanted to wake Lillian for a moment to tell her where I was going. If she woke up on her own and I was gone, she would panic. But she looked too peaceful, snuggled in my blankets, so I decided to leave a note instead. I scribbled "With Miles in the café. Be back soon" on a white piece of paper and laid it beside her pillow.

There were three light taps on the door. Glancing down, I realized I was still in my white t-shirt and sweatpants from last night. It would be chilly, so I grabbed a grey sweater from the end of my bed and threw it on before opening the door. I cracked it open just a little so Miles' blue eyes appeared in the crevice. Opening it the smallest amount possible, I slid into the hallway. As soon as I stepped out, his arms were around my waist, pulling me close. I stood on my tip toes and wrapped mine around his shoulders, just like I pictured. We were holding each other so tightly I could barely breathe, but I didn't care. He cupped my face in his hands and pressed his lips against mine hard and fast, giving me quick, urgent pecks.

"I'm so glad to see you," he whispered. He pulled me against his chest again and I turned my head so I could hear his heartbeat. Miles gently cupped my cheek and pressed his lips against the top of my head. We stayed like that, sort of swaying back and forth, for what seems like an eternity. When I pulled back, I noticed how bright it was in the hallway. Much brighter than usual. I squinted my eyes. The lighting on the wall was no longer dimmed. The administration was already taking precautions.

"Let's go to the café. I feel exposed in the hallway alone," I said.

As we walked to the café the halls were silent. Most people were still asleep or maybe scared to leave their rooms, but as we got closer to the café mumbles of conversations began drifting through the air. When we entered the café, my mouth nearly fell open. There were even more people seated at the tables than usual. On a normal Saturday morning, it would be a ghost town before nine a.m. But not today. Tables were full and every student was leaned forward invested in their own conversations about their stories from last night. Even though everyone was focused on their personal discussion, I could tell they were alert at the same time, very aware of their surroundings. As we walked in between tables, trying to find an empty seat, I watched every head turn in our direction.

Some boys and girls sat up straight as we passed by, attempting to let everyone know they shouldn't cross them. The younger students were clearly nervous, though. The girl last night could have been their friend. That would be enough to make anyone cower away from people they didn't know, especially if both of those people were at the crime scene last night.

We finally found two chairs at a tiny table towards the back of the room, close to the food bar. "Do you want anything?" Miles asked. I shook my head no, and he sat down across from me. My stomach was too nervous to think about eating. As I looked around the room, I noticed most of the tables were void of trays. Everyone was on edge this morning and food was the last thing on our minds.

"What happened last night?" I asked, hesitantly. "Did the girl…"

"I was on the way back from the bathroom when I heard her scream," he started from the beginning, his eyes staring into the distance like he was picturing himself back in the hallway. "I ran around the corner and she was on the ground.

I tried to pick her up…maybe I shouldn't have moved her. I didn't know what to do. That's when I saw her head was bleeding. It was everywhere…" He ran his fingers through his curly hair and tilted his head down in his hands. It was quiet for a moment. "I ran down the hallway and called the medical center on one of the emergency phones they keep in the corners of the hallways. They dispatched some nurses that were already close, but it was too late…" His voice trailed off. His head was still in his hands. So, the girl was gone. She didn't survive.

I reached out and put my hand over his. He wrapped both his hands round mine and lifted his head back up. "Her bones were shattered, Josie. When she fell back, or was thrown back, she cracked her head. A spell did this…" His wild eyes seared through mine.

"Someone did a spell that caused *this*?" I asked in disbelief. "How do you know?"

"I've been studying different types of magic for a while—some good and some...not so good—and I read about a spell that causes this *exact* type of damage to the body. The nurses thought it was magic, too, but they didn't know what spell." The words fell out of his mouth so quickly it was almost impossible to understand.

"Did you tell them what spell it was?" I asked, flashing back to the black book on his nightstand again.

"Not at first," he admitted as if he were ashamed. "I was scared, Josie. I didn't want them to think I had done it. And there's a book in my room with that exact spell in it. But I was talking to the Headmistress in the medical wing for hours. I couldn't leave the girl with no answers. She deserved some justice. When they still couldn't figure it out, I told one of the nurses what I thought it could be. The Headmistress recognized the spell right away. Maybe she knew the whole time and was waiting to see if I would crack. They had their cause of death, then. You can't survive a spell like *that*."

"Why would you be scared they would think it was you? You called for help, Miles. You did nothing wrong," I tried to reassure him even though my words couldn't fix what happened.

"You know what others assume about witches who study dark magic. If that's your major at North End, people don't want to associate with you. They're scared you're a Follower or a witch gone bad. I don't want anyone to think of me that way. I don't *just* study dark magic," he whispered, glancing over his shoulder to make sure no one was listening to our conversation. "I just wanted to know as much as I could. And...I didn't think it was a bad idea to be able to protect myself from those sorts of evil. My family history hasn't been simple."

"What do you mean?" I asked, confused. "Are you in

danger?"

"No, no. I have no reason to think I'm in immediate danger." He chose his words carefully and squeezed my hand tighter. "My mother…let's just say she wasn't Glinda the Good Witch. She joined a coven that did the Fallen Angel's bidding. That's when she left us. I assume she's still with them if she's still alive." I could tell it was hard for him to say the words. His voice hitched when he uttered "still alive."

"Miles, I am so sorry." We both lost our mothers, but for two very different reasons. At least I felt peace knowing my mother had been good.

"I'm afraid she sold her soul to him. The Fallen Angel…" He shook his head and stared blankly at the table. "I just want to be able to protect my dad and myself. And now I want to be able to protect you."

"I feel safe with you," I smiled. And I meant it. All the doubts and suspicion from last night had already faded away.

"Do you still trust me?" He looked at me with pleading eyes. "I know dark magic isn't something to take lightly. I was going to tell you about my mother, too. I just didn't know if that was really a second date conversation," he laughed darkly and looked away. "It's a lot for anyone to take in."

I put my free hand on his chin and turned his head back to face me. "I trust you," I told him with confidence. "This all feels more serious than just a second date anyway." His smile touched his eyes, then.

"It does for me, too. I want you to know every part of me." We stared into each other's eyes for a while. I was lost in them. He wanted me to know all of him, but I felt like I already knew his soul. He was good.

"Does the Headmistress believe you?" I asked, directing the conversation back to the girl. "Do they know who did this?"

"No, they have no idea who has a motive. They're sure it's someone in the building. No unauthorized person has been in the school. It could be another student…a professor even. They don't think I'm a suspect though. I spent nearly the whole night with Craw answering questions, helping them in any way I could."

"Do you know who the girl was?" I asked him, scanning the café. Who here knew the girl? Who sat beside her in class? Who shared a room with her? Who was her Lillian? And who would want to harm her?

"Her name was Laura. She was thirteen. It was her first year." I clenched my jaw as the weight of this news pushed down on my chest like a boulder. It was hard to catch my breath. She was in her first year. I remembered myself at that age. I had the perfect family. I was full of hope and wonder as I stepped foot on the island for the first time, the same hope and wonder Laura surely felt on her first day here, just a few months ago. She was still a child. "They don't know much about her. She was only at school for a few months. Her family is a small, unproblematic few. It doesn't make any sense."

I thought of the young girl, who I now knew to be Laura, on the floor. Her hair was long and blonde. She was petite, even more so than Lillian. She was in her pajamas. Yellow. The color of first year students. She barely had a chance to live. She didn't even have her powers for more than a couple of years at most.

"What kind of spell was used exactly?" I asked. Miles bit his lip like he didn't want to tell me.

We were interrupted by the crackle of the intercom. "Good morning, students. This is Headmistress Craw. There will be a mandatory meeting for all grade levels in the auditorium in the North Wing in 30 minutes. All students must be present. Thank you."

Miles squeezed my hand twice then stood from his seat. "We should head over. It'll be crowded with every student in the school heading that way." The café was already starting to clear out. Most students were standing and walking towards the exit that led towards the North Wing. I stood and took his hand as we followed the crowd through the exit.

* * *

The auditorium was seldom used. There weren't many times the school had enough people in one place to require such a large space. It was always full on graduation, but I had never attended one. The only time I'd been inside it was my first day here. Walking down the hallway to the entrance took me back to that day. Each year new students would come with their families to the First Year Ceremony. My parents insisted we arrive early that day. We ended up in the third row, so close to the front and center. The Headmistress had spoken, as well as a few professors, including Professor Rose. My mom spoke, too. She was always involved in things that were important to the school. And since she was in line to be the next Headmistress, Craw thought it appropriate for her to say a few words. She talked about the years she spent at the school, how she discovered her powers, and how they developed through hard work and discipline. She didn't speak of her powerful bloodline. She wanted each student to know they all had the chance to be powerful if they wanted to. I was glad to be sitting in the third row that day. I beamed with pride watching her speak so passionately about what she loved. She would have been the perfect Headmistress.

Nerves were eating my stomach that first day, but I hadn't been immune to the excitement in the air. The mood was completely different this time. When we stepped through the doors, hand in hand, the tension was palpable. Some first years were crying. Others had their arms around each other in efforts to comfort one another; to make each other feel safe. Like an ineffective security blanket. No one could protect you from the unknown. No one was safe until this mystery was solved. People wanted answers that nobody had except one person who would be in this room with all of us: the murderer.

The auditorium was just as big as I remembered. The ceilings were as tall as the ones in the library, but instead of glass at the top there were only steel rafters. I would have preferred the glass ceilings. The steel bars made me feel trapped. Would the person who committed this cold-blooded crime feel trapped, too? Or were they proud of themselves? Were they wrapped around their friends emitting faux tears for the sake of appearances? Or were they sitting alone in a back row, unbothered by the hysteria around them? Surely they were smart enough to at least pretend to be sad, keeping the smug look off their face in public.

The room had stadium seating with five different sections of seats, each higher than the last. The bottom section was already filled so we went up to the next one. As we sat down, I scanned the crowd searching for Lillian. Miles, knowing I needed my best friend right now, began looking for her, too.

"Hey, there she is!" he exclaimed. I followed where he was pointing and saw her climbing up the steps to our section with Ava and Daliah behind her. I jumped up and waved my arms.

"Lillian!" I called out over the shuffling of students. I watched her eyes survey the crowd until she found me and waved. Relief flooded her face. There was only one seat beside us, so she crossed the crowd, and our two roommates continued up the steps to more seating.

"Thank the Divinity I found you!" she whispered, wrapping her arms around me. "I was worried when I woke up and you were gone." We took our seats beside each other with Miles on the other side of me. "Hi Miles," Lillian waved, putting on her friendliest face.

"Hey, Lillian. Thank you for coming to get our girl last night." I saw Lillian raise one eyebrow out of the corner of my eye and I tried to hide my smile. *Our* girl. Now probably wasn't the time to be smiling like a schoolgirl over a boy. "I hated leaving her in my room. Everything was so chaotic."

"I can't imagine, but we're all here for each other," she said, giving my shoulders a squeeze. We sat quietly while the remainder of the school filed in. There were a few whispers, but for the most part groups of people were sitting silently. I guess no one knew what to say.

Once everyone was seated Headmistress Craw headed for the microphone in the middle of the stage. By the time she took her third step, the room was dead silent; the only noise were the heels of Headmistress Craw's shoes clicking on the hardwood floor. I had never seen a group of people this big be so quiet. Two guards followed closely behind Craw. They were the two tallest men I had ever seen, surely towering above seven foot, and made of pure muscle. It was clear why she had chosen *these* guards to stand with her on stage. No professors accompanied her, and I wondered if that was for their own safety or because the whole staff, along with the student body, was under speculation.

Craw stopped in front of the microphone. She stood silently for a moment, taking in the crowd, then closed her eyes as if contemplating how to start.

"Students," she began, her voice calm, almost soothing. "I'm aware that most of you have already heard about the tragedy that struck our school last night. A first year student named Laura Hodge died. I cannot divulge much about the event, but you deserve to know the truth. We have reason to believe there was foul play." I could feel the air leave the room even though most of the students already had this theory in their minds. Actually, hearing the words come from Craw's mouth made it final, set in stone, like a nightmare come to life within our home, the place we all used to feel safe. I saw people in all black moving to my left side. It startled me and I turned to see several guards, almost as large as the two behind Craw, making their way through all the aisles beside our seats. They were wearing earpieces and scanning the crowd inconspicuously. "We don't have much information to share. I know you must have questions, but right now I'm encouraging you *not* to ask them, for we do not have many answers. Please do not be alarmed. You are under the best care possible. We have called in for more guards. They will all be here tonight. There will be enough to be placed in almost every hallway in the dormitory sections of the school. I *will* make sure this does not happen again. You will be safe."

Miles put his hand on my leg and looked at me as if to say he would also keep me safe. I trusted his word more than Craw's, even though I knew deep down that if someone in this school was using dark magic like this there would be no one that could stop them. Maybe not even Craw.

"We will be taking extra precautions in the upcoming days." She paused and swallowed hard. "As we speak, several guards and *trusted* employees are searching your rooms for any clues that may help..." Her voice was difficult to hear over the murmurs that were erupting throughout the crowd. Lillian and I looked at each other and, even though neither of us had anything to hide, clearly felt uneasy. It seemed like a complete invasion of privacy, but at the same time I was relieved that we would surely have some answers after the search. There was nothing we could do to stop the school from searching our rooms anyway. We were powerless here. And privacy wasn't something we were entitled to at a time like this.

"Josie," I heard Miles whisper. "That book is in my

room." I looked over to see his face filled with terror. "The book with the spell used by the murderer."

"The book with dark magic…" I whispered, feeling his terror spread to my face. "Hold on, though. You told Craw about the spell. She knows—"

"I didn't tell her I had a book like that in my room. Only that I'd heard of the spell." His voice shook.

"It's okay. It'll be okay. Craw trusts you. She knew you had to get the spell from somewhere," I reassured him. I was sure that was true, but unsure why I still felt a pit deep in my stomach. After all the help Miles gave them last night, they couldn't suspect him.

"It just looks bad," he hissed, looking away. "Especially with my family history…" Headmistress Craw held one hand in the air as a signal for us all to stop talking. The crowd was silenced instantly.

"I understand your concern. Some may argue this is an invasion of privacy, but that does not mean this invasion isn't necessary at this moment." She went on to discuss the precautions the school would be taking. It basically sounded like we needed to get used to more security, walking in pairs, and living by the motto "if you see something, say something." Half an hour ticked by while Craw and the guards continued their speeches and I started to suspect they were only being this detailed so our rooms could be searched in full.

When we were finally dismissed, the auditorium erupted with voices. The mood was completely different than it was when we entered. People were angry. Some even frantic.

"I have devil's juice in my room!" I overheard a tall girl with light red hair exclaim to her friend in a panicked voice.

Her friend slung her brown hair over her shoulder nonchalantly and rolled her eyes. "What would that have to do with a murder?"

"They could make a connection somehow!" the girl with the red hair exclaimed as she fought her way through the crowd in a rush to get back to her room.

The meeting didn't give us the answers we hoped for. Most students were practically shoving their way out of the auditorium, but the three of us just sat, waiting for the crowd to clear.

"You okay?" I whispered to Miles so Lillian couldn't hear. I knew it wasn't something Miles wanted people to know. I could already tell he thought no one would understand.

"Yeah. Just anxious to get back to my room now. I need to see if the book is gone," he whispered back. I noticed his knee was quickly bouncing up and down. I placed my hand on it to slow it. Eventually, the crowd died down and we all stood.

"Do you want me to come with you?" I asked. He just shook his head, bent down to kiss my cheek and said he would see me later. Then he made his way towards the exit.

"Everything okay?" Lillian's purple eyes were wide with worry.

"Yeah, it's fine," I smiled, trying to push my concern deep down. "He just wanted to meet up with his roommates. You want to head back to the room?"

"Sure," she said as we walked down the stairs. "Isn't it kind of messed up that they can search our rooms whenever they want?"

"I guess so. They just want answers like we do. The messed-up part is that this is the only way they can get them. They must have no leads." I shuddered at the thought that they were as clueless as us.

We crossed campus to our dorm room, passing several guards on the way. Once we made it inside it looked virtually untouched. "Did anyone even search our room?" Lillian scoffed, confused. "We lifted the protection spell before we left so they should have been able to get in…"

"I have no idea," I said as I picked up a crumpled sweater that was in the exact location I left it at the foot of my bed. "Maybe they're just really good at making it seem like they were never here. They could search our rooms all the time for all we know."

"Well, search away guards! There's nothing to find in our room except schoolbooks and my journal. We're so boring," Lillian giggled.

"We follow all the rules," I giggled, too. "No murder weapons or anything! Snoozefest." The two of us decided to hang out in our room for the rest of the afternoon. Craw had discouraged us from spending unnecessary time wandering the campus and we had no reason to leave anyway. Not many people were planning any parties at the moment. It wasn't a usual Saturday afternoon at North End.

Ava and Daliah made it back soon after us, and Ava seemed offended that our room looked unsearched. "Do they think we're not capable of doing bad things? Like we don't have enough power or something?"

Lillian argued that the administrators trusting us was a good thing while she pulled up a movie on her small laptop. We all gathered to watch it. The girls spent a majority of the movie chatting and continuing their argument about the room search, and I spent a majority of it glancing in the direction of my phone. With each minute that passed, my stomach knotted more.

Six o'clock rolled around and I still hadn't heard from Miles. I tried to rationalize it in my head. *He was vague when he said he would talk to me later. He didn't set a specific time. Maybe he's just with his friends. Or maybe he went to talk to Headmistress Craw about the book. He doesn't have to talk to me all day every single day.* But even as I played these explanations on a loop in my head, I knew deep down that if Miles could have called me then he would have. I thought about how panicked he looked when Craw said the guards would be searching rooms and knew my worries were much more serious than those of a clingy girlfriend. He could actually be in danger.

When another half hour passed, I decided I would call *him*. I rolled over to my bed and dialed the number. It only took three rings for him to pick up.

"Hello?" he said with a low, husky voice.

"Hey!" I squealed. Relief washed over me. He was okay. "Can I see you?" I asked hopefully. That hope was instantly squashed, and my relief started to trickle away. Replacing it were the same knots in my stomach from earlier.

"I can't really talk right now. I'm in Craw's office." There were long pauses between his sentences. "They found the book." I stayed silent. So, he hadn't gone there voluntarily. They found the book and called him in for questioning. I felt the blood drain from my face.

"Josie?" he whispered anxiously.

"Are you okay? Do they think you're a suspect?" I whispered, knowing he couldn't explain if he was in Craw's office, but unable to stop the words from pouring out.

"I got to go," he said abruptly, and the phone went silent. I could feel my heart pounding through my whole body.

"What's going on?" Lillian asked when I returned to the group. Three sets of eyes stared at me. I tried not to make eye contact as I lied and said "nothing," but I could feel Lillian's glare burning a hole in the side of my head. She *knew* something was going on, but she also knew better than to ask again in front of an audience. She didn't push further, but I would have to have a conversation with her later. I hoped she would understand Miles' situation. Would she think he was a suspect, too? Or would she trust me when I said he was innocent?

6
UP ALL NIGHT

The night had come and gone, but it hadn't passed slowly. I tossed and turned uncontrollably, getting almost no sleep. I must have checked my phone 10 times for a call from Miles, but no call ever came. I rolled over in bed to face Lillian. She was already awake and reading a book with the curtain cracked open. I looked at the clock on the wall. It was 9:05. I had slept more than I thought. The last time I checked the clock showed 5:50. I still felt weak and achy, though. Not only did my body feel tired, my mind did, too. The thought of Miles stuck in Craw's office didn't leave my head all night. Even when I actually fell asleep, I was startled awake by dreams of the black book or Craw screaming at Miles. The worst of the dreams portrayed Miles as the villain. That one kept me up for over an hour.

I thought morning might bring some sense of clarity or relief, but instead of a new day it just felt like yesterday kept going. Lillian noticed me moving underneath the covers and turned to face me.

"Did you sleep at all last night?" she murmured. Either she heard me tossing and turning or I looked exhausted. It was probably both.

"I don't even know," I groaned. Lillian peaked over her shoulder at Ava and Daliah. Ava was snoring and Daliah lay flat on her back with her mouth wide open.

"What's going on, Josie?" she asked now that she knew it was safe. I double checked to see if either roommate had moved. They hadn't. So, I told her everything while keeping my voice low: all about the black book I found before the scream, how Miles was the one that led them to the spell that killed Laura, and finally about how they found the black book during the search. I stopped there since I didn't have any more information, only speculation and worry.

"Do you believe him?" she asked seriously.

"Yes," I answered confidently. "I really do, Lillian. The way I feel when I'm with him...I can't explain it. I haven't felt this safe since I lost Mom. He couldn't hurt anyone that way."

She paused to take in what I said. "Then, I believe him, too."

"You do?" I asked, peeking at her through my eyelashes.

"Yes," she whispered undoubtedly. "I don't think you could love a murderer. You have good instincts. And there's something about Miles. Even *I* feel like I can trust him, and I barely know the boy."

Relief washed over me. I was so worried that I was being foolish and would be blindsided by a truth that I refused to see, but if Lillian believed in Miles then I knew I could, too. However, I was still stuck on one of Lillian's words.

"I never said I *loved* him," I mumbled, feeling suddenly shy. I ran my fingers through my hair nervously.

"You didn't have to." She smirked, then turned over to continue reading her book. I thought about the word "love" for a moment. I'd certainly never been in love before. I'd dated a few boys, but it was never anything remotely serious for either party. My feelings *were* very strong. But did that mean it was love? I wasn't sure yet. I grew up seeing the way my mom and dad looked at each other, how they treated each other. They were the perfect example of true love. Watching them from a young age programmed me to never settle for less than what they had. What would my mom think about Miles if she were here to meet him? I wished more than anything she could give me her opinion on love.

I tried to carry on through the day with as much normalcy as I could muster, but there was a constant gnawing in my stomach. I forced myself to shower and when I returned to our room Ava and Daliah were awake. The four of us went to the café to have brunch, still wearing our pajamas. The temperature had risen slightly so we ate outside on the balcony at my favorite spot. I picked at a bagel, but when everyone had finished their food, most of the bagel was in pieces scattered on my plate.

"I wish I could pull off short hair like her," Ava mused as she eyed the first year student at the table closest to us. Her hair was a similar shade to Ava's but was cut shoulder length.

"I like your hair just fine," Daliah said before taking a sip of her orange juice.

I heard the door to the balcony open and Professor Rose stepped out. The wind blew back her grey hair, making her look as beautiful as ever, and I leaned forward to see whose hand was holding the door open for her. Professor Howard stepped into the sunlight. They walked to the edge of the balcony together. Professor Rose wore a smile on her pink lips as she spoke to him. When she leaned forward onto the railing, he placed his hand on the back of her white dress.

"You know, I heard they were *together*," Daliah whispered and I noticed she was looking at Professor Rose and Professor Howard, too. Lillian turned all the way around in her seat to gaze at them.

"Don't look!" Ava hissed, using her long red hair as shield to peak through without being caught staring at the pair.

"They're not paying attention to us anyway," Lillian said. Ava rolled her eyes. "Look at his hand! Maybe they *are* together."

"No way," I objected. Professor Howard was gorgeous, but I could tell from our meetings he and Professor Rose would not be a match. Professor Rose radiated light and carried herself with such grace. She worshiped the Divinity. Not to mention her brilliance. Not that Professor Howard wasn't brilliant in his own right, but nothing like Rose. Plus, his office was decorated with the Fallen Angel, and I had a feeling he wasn't above using dark magic. Professor Rose seemed to have high standards in all avenues of her life. She wouldn't settle for less than perfection. And, even though I liked him as a professor and a mentor, Howard just didn't meet that description.

"I'm serious," Daliah whispered. "A guy in my Elemental class said he saw Professor Rose leave Howard's room in the middle of the night a few weeks ago. It was obviously not a school-related meeting." She raised her eyebrows and smirked.

Just then Professor Rose laughed so loudly we heard it on the other side of the balcony. Rose turned to gaze at the view, but Howard's eyes didn't leave her face.

"Hmmm," I pondered. "He is really giving her the eyes, isn't he?" Maybe they were an item and my instincts weren't as spot on as Lillian claimed. "Why would they keep it a secret?"

"They probably don't want kids like us gossiping about their personal lives all day," Lillian laughed.

"We'll talk anyway. There isn't much else to do on this island," Ava mused, sighing dramatically like her life was such a bore. She placed her chin on her hands and gazed at Rose enviously. "I wouldn't blame Rose for wanting him. He *is* hot. Who cares who he worships?"

"Not Professor Rose, obviously," Daliah smiled. I felt guilty gossiping about someone I looked up to so much. I should probably feel guilty gossiping about anyone in general, but Rose dedicated a majority of her life to teaching teenagers like us magic. She lived at the school with us. I wanted to respect the small amount of privacy she had. The same applied to all of my professors, including Professor Howard.

"Well, hello ladies," Professor Howard proclaimed over my shoulder, appearing out of thin air. I turned around slowly to greet him and prayed he hadn't heard our conversation. Ava and Daliah clearly had the same fear I did. Daliah cheeks were red and Ava was twirling her hair around her finger.

"Hello, Professor Howard," we said in unison.

"How are you on this fine day?" Professor Howard asked.

"Just fine. How are you?" I responded.

"Oh, I'm dandy. What were you ladies discussing?" My heart thudded and my words got caught in my throat. He had heard us. I tried to think of something else—anything else—

to claim we were discussing, but my mind was blank. Thankfully, Lillian spoke up.

"Ava was just saying she wished she could pull off short hair," Lillian shrugged easily.

Professor Howard looked Ava up and down before saying, "You would look dashing with short hair, Ava." Ava blushed deeply, and Howard winked at me slyly before turning around to return to Professor Rose by the balcony.

"You guys ready?" I asked abruptly, standing before they could answer. I didn't want to risk Howard hearing anymore of our conversations. That encounter was uncomfortable enough.

"Sure," Lillian said. We all gathered our trays and trash and we walked into the café.

As we made our way to the exit, after dumping our trays, I saw Miles walking right towards us. Lillian saw him, too, and glanced at me out of the corner of her eye. My face told her what she needed to know. "Let's head back to the room and give these two love birds some privacy," she suggested. The three of them disappeared around the corner, but I heard Ava giggling all the way down the hall. Miles smiled as soon as I moved towards him. The dark circles under his eyes were prominent, like he hadn't slept at all. He quickened his pace to close the distance between us. When he finally made it to me, he lifted me up and swung me around, burying his face in my hair. When my feet hit the floor again, I noticed several students staring at us and my cheeks flushed pink. I guess we were officially public now. If this many people saw us, the whole school would soon know we were together. Like Ava said, there wasn't much to do on this island besides talk.

"Hey," he laughed. How could he be in such a good mood if he was as exhausted as he looked?

"Hey," I responded, feeling the anxiety drift away and the wholeness fill my chest. I had never been more relieved to see someone. "Are you okay?" I leaned forward brushing the dark spots under his eyes and placing my hands on his cheeks. He enveloped my hands in his and kissed each of them.

"I'm better now." It looked like he meant it. Like this feeling that filled my chest was filling his, too. I tore my eyes away from his for the first time since I saw him cross the room and realized right away that he was still wearing the clothes he had on when he left me yesterday.

"You look exhausted," I said, stating the obvious.

"I am. I haven't been asleep since I saw you last," he explained while glancing over his shoulder at the people closest to us. Their table had suddenly fallen silent. They were probably listening to every word we said. "Let's talk somewhere else."

We moved our conversation back to the balcony, where only a couple students were sitting. I noticed Professor Rose and Professor Howard were no longer leaning on the railing, and I wondered if they'd gone somewhere else together. Miles chose the table furthest from the other students and sat down. I sat in the chair next to him and tucked myself under his arm. He wrapped it around my shoulder, rubbing my arm as if to keep me warm.

Miles started to explain what happened to him yesterday in a hushed tone, saying when he got back to his room after the assembly a guard was waiting for him. "He didn't even say anything when he saw me. He just held up the book and started walking down the hall. I knew to follow him. We went straight to Craw's office. She didn't seem surprised to see me." He continued, saying he had stayed up all night being questioned by the guards. Around 5:00 a.m., Craw came into the room to talk to him. "Like I said, she didn't seem surprised to see me. Like you said yesterday, she knew I read that spell *somewhere*. She asked me a lot of questions about my family and home life...mostly about my mom. I think that's why she kept me there for so long and had the guards question me first. She needed to make sure I wasn't in contact with my mother. That I wouldn't follow the Fallen Angel like she had. And like Craw had previously." He paused to take a deep breath. I could tell that talking about his mother hurt him. Even though they hadn't been close like me and my mom, he still felt abandoned.

"Whatever I told her must have convinced her I had

nothing to do with what happened. Craw let me go after that, but she didn't give my book back. She warned me to never mess with that magic again because it can turn even the best witches into something bad, even if they don't want to go there, even if they don't realize what's happening. I wonder if that's what happened to her, if that's how she got mixed in with the Fallen Angel."

"Maybe she's right, Miles," I offered, delicately choosing my words, so he knew I trusted him, but that I was also worried. "Who knows what reading all those spells does to your mind." His expression changed and I worried he felt like I wasn't on his side. "I just want you to be careful. If something bad happened to you I don't know if I could take it." I had suffered enough loss for a lifetime. I couldn't handle the boy I was falling for turning into a Follower.

"I appreciate you saying that. And you're right. No more dark magic." Miles was quiet then, looking out at the tall grass swaying the wind. I was more interested in the view in front of me, watching his curls dance as the breeze blew through them. He looked back at me and smiled suddenly before tucking a piece of hair behind my ear. "On a different note…" he said in a lighter tone, still smiling.

"What?" I asked nervously, leaning back and narrowing my eyes.

"I've been meaning to ask you something, and last night I

was terrified I would be locked away without having the chance to do it. I won't let this moment escape me again. So, Josie Grace Parker, would you go to the Hallow's Eve dance with me?" He basically yelled this part of the conversation, making sure the two students on the balcony, and maybe even some inside the café, could hear his words. I blushed a deep red when people turned to look at us, but loved every second of it. He was proud to be with me.

"Yes," I whispered, giggling.

"She said 'yes!' She said 'yes!'" He cheered, lifting his hands in the arm and standing. He picked me up from my chair and twirled me around again.

"This is ridiculous!" I giggled. And it was. But I had never loved something so ridiculous the way I loved this moment.

7
A NEW NORMAL

The next few days came and went without anything out of the ordinary happening. On Sunday, everyone was still anxious—like we were standing on the edge of a cliff knowing someone was coming to push us off, but unable to watch their approach. We were all sure another attack was approaching. But it never did. By Thursday, everyone was a little more at ease; not fully relaxed, but less tense than before.

We continued going to our classes and doing our homework. Life went on, and by Friday, I could tell everyone was almost back to normal, with the exception of a few first year students. It was strange how quickly people seemed to forget the danger. The guards still stood in most hallways and the absence of the young girl, Laura, was still there, but people were doing what they had to do. The school held a memorial service for Laura on Monday night. We stood on the front lawn of the school, each holding a small, white candle in our hands. I'd bet every single student in the school was there. Even though we didn't all know her, she was part of us, part of our family. We felt protective of each other even if we weren't best friends. Despite the fact that most were carrying on like normal, we were all aware of the fact that it could have easily been one of us, and this knowledge created a unity at the school like I had never seen before.

Headmistress Craw also had a huge flower arrangement placed in the garden. It was filled with tropical leaves and neon flowers that were native to Laura's home country. It stood out from all the green. Her school picture was placed in the middle of the arrangement. I saw it every day as I walked to class. She wore her school colors and smiled a somewhat forced smile for the camera while posing in front of a black background. Her hair was twisted in a perfect French braid. I wished they had chosen a different picture. Maybe a silly one her friend had taken of her laughing or one of her off guard at the café. I wanted to know more about what she was really like, but the school photo didn't leave much room for personality. Still, it was the only reminder that even though things *seemed* normal in my small world, they would never be the same. Not for the girl or her family. Not for our school. And the mystery remained. There were still no answers for the thousands of questions about Laura's incomprehensible death.

In my world, Miles and I grew closer. Quickly. Perhaps it was because of how strong our connection naturally was. Maybe it was because we had gone through a tragic event recently. Probably a little of both. Whatever the reason was, I felt closer to Miles than I had ever felt to someone. All of the things I loved about him while we were just friends were amplified. His sense of humor, his kindness, his smile, how open he was. We spent nearly every second of our free time together that week.

However, I reserved Saturday night for Lillian. She wanted to go dress shopping for the Hallow's Eve dance next Friday. Our tiny island didn't have shops of any kind though, so a few times a year when a special occasion was coming up the school would bring in a shop. They used one of the rooms near the opening of the school and once you walked in you didn't feel like you were at school anymore. Instead you were stepping into a real boutique. It reminded me of shopping with my mom, who was basically a shopping addict. When I was growing up, we would spend hours of our weekends visiting shop after shop, looking for unique items that neither of us truly needed. I was glad Lillian was also a shopping addict because I missed those days with my mom, and this was as close to them as I would get.

"I really want something that *pops* this year!" Lillian said as we entered the shop. There were white curtains hanging everywhere, despite the fact that there were no windows in the room, and too many racks to count. All the dresses in my line of sight appeared to be high end, and I immediately knew there was no way I would be able to afford one.

"You always wear something that pops," I teased. My dad usually sent me spending money every other month. It wasn't much, but it was all we could afford since he was never able to return to work after the accident. He must have forgotten the past few months, though, and my funds were running low. I could have called to remind him, but the inevitable silence on the other end wasn't really worth the money to buy some random dress. I could just wear an old one hanging in my closet or maybe Ava had one I could borrow. We were about the same size.

Now I couldn't help but picture my dad sitting in his armchair wearing his grey robe. Alone. The TV would be on, but he wouldn't really be paying attention. Just staring into space. That's what I came home to each summer. Nothing ever changed. Thankfully, the house was always as neat and organized just as I had left it, like it was frozen in time. Not because my dad spent time cleaning, but because it was like no one lived there at all. The only way to tell any time had passed was to look at the dust collecting on top of the surfaces. I cringed away from the thought and realized I had been zoned out of the conversation with Lillian. I tried to tune back in. "—like, not *revealing*, but different. You know what I mean?" She was fanning through her second rack of dresses rather quickly, completely passing over any neutral colors.

"Mmhm," I mumbled. She glanced over at me, disapproving of my apathetic attitude. "Sorry," I sighed. I hated sucking the joy out of the things Lillian loved. "My mind is just...somewhere else I guess."

"You of all people should be excited for this dance. You actually have a date you like. I'm going dateless once again without even my best friend to comfort me." She put her palm over her forehead and leaned back like she was feeling faint from the idea.

I rolled my eyes. "You are obviously going to hang out with us the whole night. I have two dates this year."

"Lucky you!" She started forming a small pile of options on her right arm while continuing the search with her left. "Can you help me out, please?" she asked as she reached me a neon yellow, ruffled dress.

"Really? This one?" I questioned, raising my eyebrows as I held it in front of me. It looked like a horrible bridesmaid dress from the 80's.

"I want to try everything! Aren't you going to try on something?" I thought about lying, coming up with some other reason for not buying a new dress and rewearing an older one that would probably be slightly snug, but Lillian wouldn't buy it. So, I opted for the truth.

"I don't have the money right now. So, I'm just going to wear one of my old ones." I shrugged.

"No, no, no." Here we go. An offer to pay for my dress. I knew it came from a place of love, but nothing made me more uncomfortable. Her family had already spent more money on me than I could count. They were especially generous when my mom passed away. "Let me get you something. Seriously. I have leftover money this month anyway."

"No, Lillian," I said more sternly than I meant to. "I don't need a whole new dress anyway." Lillian was quiet for a moment, probably contemplating pushing the situation further, but she decided against it.

"Well, here, at least try a few on with me so I don't feel lonely. Then, if you decide you love one, I can get it for you." She said this as she held up a gorgeous, black dress. I couldn't resist. I was weak.

"I'll try it on, but you are *not* buying it." Lillian nodded like she understood. She handed me the dress and we headed to the changing rooms. I knew she would truly love to buy me the dress. She would never hold it against me or act as if I owed her something. Lillian was a true friend. We were really like family now, and family helped each other out. But it wasn't

Lillian's fault my mother was gone and my father was unstable. She had big plans after school and she needed to save her money for the future, not blow it on a dress that wasn't even for her. Just for a silly dance. So, I needed to be a true friend in return and make sure she planned for her future that held endless possibilities.

I slipped the dress over my head and posed in front of the dressing room mirror. It *was* stunning. I tried not to stare too long. I would not be swayed. "Are you ready?" Lillian yelled from her dressing room.

"Yep!" I stepped out and turned to face Lillian but was met with a different face. Professor Rose stood in front of the mirror in a dress she was trying on. It was a floor length, deep blue gown with pearls splattered on the long sleeves. She turned her attention to me when I stepped out.

"Good evening, Ms. Parker. Oh my, that is quite a dress!" she exclaimed, placing her hand delicately on her chest as if she were genuinely taken aback.

"Thank you, Professor Rose." I felt my cheeks turn a shade of pink. Lillian popped out from behind Professor Rose in her yellow, frilly disaster.

"Hi, Professor Rose," Lillian said as she bopped out of the dressing room before coming to a halt in front of me. "Whoa! Josie, you look gorgeous!"

"Give us a spin, darling," Professor Rose suggested as she

delicately waved her hand in a circle. I obliged shyly, spinning slowly and avoiding direct eye contact. "Is this for the Hallow's Eve dance?"

"Oh...uh, no. I'm just here to support Lillian on her shopping venture." I pointed to Lillian and tried to freeze my face into a neutral expression as I took in her dress. Professor Rose was having a difficult time controlling her face, as well.

"Oh my! That dress..." Professor Rose drifted off, unable to find the words to describe the yellow frill.

"I know! I know!" Lillian exclaimed, holding up her hands. "I'm just trying a bunch of different things." She stepped in front of the mirror and twirled on her toes. "This is obviously not a winner," she laughed. The dress practically swallowed her whole. "But *that*," she turned to point to me, "is a winner. We're getting it."

"No, Lillian, you're not buying this." I tried to avoid looking in the mirror, afraid that if I looked at the dress too long, I would cave.

"Fine!" she exclaimed, frustrated. "I can't stay in this dress any longer. I'm suffocating. Next one coming up!" She hiked up the fabric that dragged the floor and hopped back into her dressing room, closing the curtain behind her.

"That truly is a stunning gown, Ms. Parker," Rose commented, her voice as soft as satin.

"Thank you. Look at yours!" I motioned towards her to

take the attention off me. "Are you shopping for the dance, too?" I asked.

"Just shopping in general, really. It is a shame there are no shops on this island. It's a rare occasion I am able to purchase something new," she mused as she turned in the mirror. "Come here, dear, take a look." She waved for me to step in front of the mirror. I may be able to argue with Lillian, but I certainly could not argue with Professor Rose. I reluctantly stepped in front of the mirror and took in the dress. The black did look good with my dark hair and made my green eyes stand out even more so than usual. Professor Rose stood behind me beaming. "Do you love it?"

"It's beautiful," I shook my head, "but I can't afford it. Lillian is offering, but I know she doesn't have that much money to spare. She needs to save it." I stepped away from the mirror and walked back to my dressing room. "I have some older dresses I can wear anyway so it's not a big deal."

"You will look radiant in whatever you choose. Have a lovely night," she waved and walked back to her dressing room.

* * *

After several failed attempts, Lillian finally found her perfect dress and skipped all the way to our room, ecstatic. When we walked in, we saw Daliah and Ava doing each other's makeup on Ava's bed. They were dressed to the nines. There must be a party tonight.

"Hey, girls!" Lillian sang. "Got my dress!" She held up the hanger which was covered in black satin to protect the dress underneath.

"Let's see it!" Daliah stopped applying blush to Ava's cheeks and stood up to jump on the bed. Ava rolled her eyes like she was too cool to worry about Lillian's dress when, in fact, she was probably the one who cared about it the most. If someone had something better than she did, she was riddled with jealousy.

"No way!" Lillian cried, rushing to hang the dress in her closet. "I want it to be a surprise! But, trust me, it's to *die* for." Daliah stopped jumping, I raised an eyebrow, and Ava turned around to shoot her a disappointed look. "Okay, maybe that wasn't the best word choice. Sorry." She frowned. "I just meant it's really pretty."

"Where's your dress, Josie?" Ava asked as Daliah sat back down to continue applying her makeup.

"I think I'll just wear one I already have. I'm trying to be frugal," I said simply. My family problems weren't something I discussed with my other two roommates. I'm not sure they would understand.

"A repeat dress?" Ava asked in a disgusted tone. I saw

NORTH END: THE BLACK FOREST

Daliah mouth "shut up" out of the corner of my eye.

"I think a repeat dress sounds fine! You already have some pretty ones," Daliah offered, even though I am sure she was not actually a fan of repeats. She was just trying to be nice. I appreciated the gesture even if it wasn't her true opinion. I shot a small smile her way before plopping down on my bed.

"Do you two want to go to a party tonight?" Ava asked with excitement.

Lillian looked at me to judge my face. A party wasn't the exact place I wanted to be tonight—I would much prefer to be wrapped up in Miles' arms—but I had reserved this night for Lillian only. This was all about *her* and whatever she wanted to do. I had no doubt she'd been feeling a little neglected lately. And it was obvious by the way her eyes glittered that she wanted to go. So, I painted a half smile on my face because if she saw any sign of resistance from me, she would never accept the invitation.

"That sounds fun," I shrugged casually. Lillian raised her eyebrow as if questioning my intentions, but it was too late. Daliah was already cheering and Ava offered to do Lillian's makeup right away so her attention was turned elsewhere before she could say another word to me.

"Thanks, Ava," Lillian smiled, and I shoved my face into a book before Lillian could examine me with her eyes any further.

* * *

The party was in a dorm belonging to a final year witch. Her parents apparently donated some special wing in the library at school, so she had one of the biggest rooms I had ever seen with only one other roommate as opposed to the usual three. The donation was supposed to be hush hush since she was obviously getting special treatment because of it, but, as usual, people love to talk. Even if they didn't, it would be obvious as soon as you set foot in the dorm. It even had a private bathroom connected.

"I didn't even know rooms like this existed," I mumbled as we made our way through the door.

Since it was twice as big as my room with only two beds, I had a feeling it was a hot spot for parties and gatherings. There were at least 20 people inside and it wasn't even crowded. Daliah and Ava led the way through the room. They bopped from group to group introducing us. Lillian struck up a quick, friendly conversation with pretty much every person we met, but I held back. I wasn't great at small talk with strangers, which was the main reason a party had not sounded like my cup of tea.

We had made our way around the whole party and were only left with one group of three older girls who were perched up close to the bathroom with black plastic cups in their hands.

Judging by Ava's reaction to the tall red headed one, she was the host of this party. Ava bounced her way over to the girl with her arms stretched wide as I realized I recognized her from somewhere. The girl squealed when she saw Ava and stretched out her arms, as well. They wrapped them around each other and bounced in a little circle. The tall girl held her cup high in the air, being very careful not to spill any of her liquid onto Ava's dress.

"Ava! It has been too long!" she cried as she pulled away from the hug. She glanced back, passed over Lillian and I, not recognizing us, and headed straight for Daliah. Neither of their reactions were quite as dramatic.

"Hello, Daliah! How are you?" the host asked, snaking one arm around her shoulders, while holding her cup in the air again. She was a head taller than Daliah.

"Hi, Crystal! What a great party!" Daliah cheered. She spoke in a weird voice that almost sounded fake. Kind of like how Ava sounded most of the time, but Daliah didn't usually talk like that around us. It was strange to hear, and I wondered why she felt like she had to put on an act for this particular group of people.

"Oh, isn't it?" Crystal responded in a high-pitched voice. "I was a little worried to host tonight—you know, with everything that's been going on. I didn't want to be the next one to wind up dead on the floor!" She laughed wildly like

Laura's death was all some practical joke someone pulled. I instinctively stepped back from the group, feeling an unusual reaction move through my body. I wasn't sure what type of person would use a young girl's death as party banter, but I knew I wanted nothing to do with someone like that. I recognized the unusual feeling in my stomach as disgust.

Ava laughed wildly along with Crystal, but the rest of us stood silently, awkwardly. "Oh, come on! Lighten up! It's just a joke," Crystal defended herself and tucked her light red hair behind her ear.

"Um...this is Lillian and Josie. They're our roommates," Daliah said in an attempt to change the subject. Crystal reached her hand out to shake both of ours.

"Ladies, it is a pleasure to meet you," she said in a formal tone.

"It's nice to meet you, too," Lillian said. I nodded but kept quiet. "Thanks for letting us tag along with Ava and Daliah. Your room is incredible." Lillian spoke with such ease. I would have been wracking my brain to think of *anything* to talk about, but not Lillian. She could strike up a conversation with anyone, even someone like Crystal.

"Isn't it the best? Thanks, daddy," she smiled and took another swig from her cup.

"What are you drinking?" Ava asked and winked.

Crystal glanced over both of her shoulders as if she was

about to tell us something top secret. She leaned in closer before whispering "This is a diabolus mix." She didn't elaborate any further and I wondered if I was the only one who was confused.

"Is that some sort of alcohol?" Lillian asked hesitantly.

"No," Crystal rolled her eyes and giggled, still whispering. "You really don't know what diabolus mix is?"

We all shrugged with the exception of Ava, who was pretending to know what it was. I had a feeling she actually had no idea, but in her eyes lying would be better than admitting she was out of the loop. "It's devil juice." The group was suddenly very still, and it seemed like the party quieted down, but maybe that was just in my head. My heart had sunk down to my feet. I wasn't sure what devil juice was, but I knew it could not be a good thing.

Suddenly I realized where I recognized Crystal from. She was the girl in the auditorium the day Headmistress Craw made her speech about Laura's death, the one that was so concerned the administration would find her "devil's juice." They obviously hadn't found it or simply didn't care if a student had it in their possession.

"W--w…what does it do?" Daliah stammered. She looked just as nervous as I felt.

"It connects your mind to the Underworld." This was starting to sound a lot like dark magic. "It gives you a direct line to the Fallen Angel so he can send you messages, if he chooses to." Her face was lit up with excitement, like it was an honor to have communication with the Fallen Angel. I felt an intense wonder for how this juice worked, but I didn't want Crystal to mistake my curiosity for interest in trying it.

"How does that work?" Lillian asked. I knew she was feeling the same way I was: curious. She was just brave enough to ask out loud.

"I'll drink this whole cup and when I go to sleep tonight the Fallen Angel will visit me," she shrugged as if she did this all the time.

"So...he visits people every time they drink this?" Daliah asked, looking into Crystal's cup. I leaned forward just a bit to glance in the cup, as well. It was a dark liquid with bubbles on the top. It looked thick. I wondered what it would taste like but shoved that thought out of my mind quickly. I didn't want to picture myself anywhere near the juice.

"Well, some people drink it and don't see him or any visions at all, but he visits *me* every time I drink it. He shows me things." She took another sip of the thick substance.

"Like what?" I felt the words leave my mouth before I had a chance to stop myself. I didn't know why I asked. I just knew I had to learn more about the juice and the people who would willingly drink it. It was like a magnetic pull.

"Different things. Sometimes it's images from the

Underworld. Sometimes it's things that haven't yet happened in *this* world. It's unbelievable."

"Yeah, almost *completely* unbelievable," Lillian said, obviously not buying anything she was saying. Crystal didn't pick up on her sarcasm though and went on rambling about the images that came to her the last time she drank this juice. She described images of the Black Forest filled with creatures from the Underworld in such detail I could almost picture myself there among these beasts. I shivered. Either Crystal really had been visited by the Fallen Angel or she had the most vivid imagination I'd ever heard.

"So, do you have to be a Follower for the potion to work?" Daliah asked. "Since it's the Fallen Angel who gives you these visions?"

"No, I don't think so. I got the visions before I decided to be a Follower. It probably works for anyone. Or maybe the Fallen Angel just has a special connection to my mind." She winked. I shivered.

I was thankful when Crystal wrapped up her story, chugged the rest of her drink, looked at Ava and said, "I need to mingle. We'll catch up later." She walked into the growing crowd of people in her room, which had already doubled. I wasn't sure there would be room for many more people.

I stayed close to Lillian's side the rest of the night as my roommates made the rounds, chatting with people they knew from class or boys they thought were cute. I felt slightly uncomfortable, but it wasn't unbearable with Lillian there. She made sure I wasn't totally left out of the conversation without forcing me to talk too much. I wasn't sure how long we had been there, maybe an hour or so, but I was starting to get bored. My mind began drifting to Miles. I pictured his eyes in my favorite shade of blue, his hand covering mine, his arm wrapped around my shoulder, making me feel even smaller than I really was. Miles.

"...that *Miles* kid probably killed her." I was snapped out of my daydream by the mention of his name out loud, here at the party. Lillian and Daliah were distracted by their conversation with two girls they knew from class, but I immediately focused on the conversation going on right behind me. I was very careful not to turn my head, but I leaned back just a bit so I could really hear what they were saying. "Dude, he had blood on his shirt!" some boy said. My heart started pounding.

"One kid from that hallway swore he saw him hit her," another said. *No!* I yelled in my head. What they were saying was completely made up. Miles would never hit someone.

"He was smiling when he came around the corner," a familiar voice cooed. My blood was boiling now. The voice I heard belonged to Frances. I was sure. My hands started shaking as I contemplated turning around and giving her a piece of my mind right in the middle of the party. I wouldn't hold anything back.

But I knew it wouldn't do any good. That was exactly what she wanted me to do. So, instead I balled my hands into fists at my side and refused to turn around for even a second. I wouldn't give her the chance to lock eyes with me and smile her smuggest smile. She would not get the satisfaction of making me snap, despite the fact that she was lying through her teeth. I was there the night of the murder. I had seen his face when he rounded that corner. It was far from a smile. He was terrified. Traumatized.

I listened as another boy backed up the lie Frances had just told and had to gnaw on my cheek to stop myself from jumping to Miles' defense, but I bit too hard and tasted blood.

"I don't know. I'm pretty sure he was the one that went to get help. Why would he bring attention to his own crime?" a girl from the group asked. My heart rate slowed. I took a deep breath. At least someone in that group had some common sense.

"I'm telling you, the dude is messed up. He probably killed her so he could be forever young or something...like the Fallen Angel," the first voice interjected.

"He better be careful messing with dark magic like that..." the girl said. There it was again. This talk of stealing someone's youth. And they thought that's what Miles wanted. I was furious. *It is just gossip. It is just gossip.* I tried to repeat it to myself to calm down. These people didn't know Miles. They just wanted a story to talk about to make their lives seem more interesting. Their words meant nothing. But it didn't work. I was still angry even after the gossip group behind me changed the subject. I was officially partied out.

"Hey, I think I'm going to head back," I whispered to Lillian.

"What? Why?" she asked, slightly concerned. "Is something wrong?" She glanced over my shoulder at the group of gossipers and her eyes widened. "Did Frances say something?" she hissed.

"No, no," I lied. There was no reason to ruin her fun. "I'm just feeling tired."

"Do you want me to come with you?" Her eyes drifted back to the two of cute boys she and Daliah were talking to. I knew she wanted nothing more than to stay, but she would leave if I needed her.

"No way!" I said. "You stay. I'm just going to lay down anyway."

"Text me if you need me," she smiled, and I watched her return to her conversation before sliding out the door. I walked down the hall and could hear conversations floating from other rooms that were having gatherings. None were quite as loud as Crystal's room, though. I was finally starting to calm down, but my adrenaline was still going. As I passed a guard at the end of the hall, I watched him give me a funny look and wondered how red the anger had made my face.

I didn't necessarily want to go back to my quiet room alone to stare at the ceiling, but I was pretty sure Miles was with his friends tonight since I told him I reserved this night for Lillian. He'd been spending all his free time with me lately, so the last thing I wanted to do was take away from his time with friends.

I wandered through the halls aimlessly, but the silence wasn't good for me. My mind kept going back to the conversation from the party where Miles was casually accused of murder. I scoffed out loud at the idea. I replayed it over in my mind and one part started to stick out. The boy that mentioned age. And the Fallen Angel. Age seemed to a recurring theme in my life lately, and it wasn't the first time it had been mentioned in relation to Laura's murder, but it was the first time I had heard age mentioned with the Fallen Angel. I'd never heard of *him* stealing someone's age. Only Mary Langley.

I was already close to the library thanks to my wandering, so I made a last second decision to stop by. I was curious about aging and had no definite answers so now seemed like a good time to get those answers myself. One sharp right turn down the hall led me straight to the library entrance.

I walked through the archway and my eyes immediately went to the ceiling. The stars shining through took away the remnants of anger from the party and made me feel at peace. I walked to the front desk but found the large mahogany table empty. I looked all around, but there was no one in sight. Even the desks in the middle of the room were empty. Not many people were studying on a Saturday night. I waited for a few minutes to see if someone would show up to help me, but no one did. Sitting on the desk was a small, silver bell. I assumed I was supposed to ring it if I needed help, so I tried it.

Ding! The bright sound echoed through the library. It seemed to bounce off every wall, sending the noise through the whole room, even though it was only a small ring. My attention followed the sound through the empty room. Being in this huge space all alone felt spooky. When I turned back around to face the front desk, I nearly screamed. A small, wrinkled woman with grey hair pinned to the top of her head stood on the opposite side of the desk. She was so small her face was the only thing visible from behind the mahogany wall separating us.

"Oh, my apologies, dear. Did I scare yeh?" the small woman spoke with a thick Irish accent.

"Just a little," I laughed at myself for being so jumpy.

"Well, I'm Mrs. Walsh. Is there something I can help yeh find?" She wore such a warm smile that the library didn't seem

142

as creepy anymore.

"I am not exactly sure what book I'm looking for...or if a book like this even exists..." I paused, unsure of how to phrase what I was about to say. I hoped to avoid any mention of the Fallen Angel in this conversation. With all the rumors going around it was risky to even ask for a book about this at all. But I had to at least try. "I was hoping to find a book about...age. Maybe one with old stories..."

"Ah, yes. You have a hankerin' to learn some history, do yah? I think I know just the thing you need." She slipped out from behind the desk and headed for the back of the library. "This way, dear." I followed obediently as she bounded ahead of me. She was half my size, making her steps much shorter and I had to slow my pace so I wouldn't pass her. We reached the end of the library, breezing past the dreaded dark magic section, and turned right. In the back corner there was a small staircase, leading to the second floor of the library. I shuffled behind Mrs. Walsh on our way up the stairs, listening to her huff and puff, then, when we reached the top, followed her to a section in the middle. We walked through rows and rows of bookshelves, each row less lit than the last, until we reached a section so dim it was difficult to read the titles of the books. It almost seemed like the school wanted to keep this section hidden.

Mrs. Walsh grabbed a ladder with wheels on the bottom.

She rolled it down the aisle a few feet before beginning her climb to the very top. The rows were so high I was afraid she would not be able to reach what she was looking for even with the aid of the ladder. She stretched on her tiptoes until she was able to snag a book on the very top shelf. She made her way back down the ladder slowly, carefully and handed me the book.

"There we are, miss. I think this will answer any questions yeh have. Be careful, though. There are only two copies in existence." *Only two copies?* It seemed irresponsible of Mrs. Walsh to give away one of the two copies of a book to a student she did not know. I wanted to ask more, but Mrs. Walsh did not make eye contact when I took the book from her hands and scurried away before I could even open my mouth.

"She's peculiar," I whispered to myself.

I stared down at the leather book and ran my hands across the front. It felt smooth, like no one had ever opened it. The book was deep brown and bound by a tie on the side. I opened the first page and strained my eyes to read a title handwritten: *"Aging Tales of a Witching World."* A date underneath the title read 1875. *This was written in 1875?* It didn't seem worn enough to be over a century old. Perhaps it was in such pristine condition because it was hidden away in this section of the library. I could almost guarantee no student came to this dimly lit, nearly hidden area to look for books for class.

I heard a creak from a few rows away and my paranoia kicked in. I looked over both my shoulders and began a quick getaway to the exit. Even though the library was dead silent, and I was the only student in it, as far as I knew, I couldn't help but feel like there were eyes on me...following me. I practically ran to the stairs and nearly tumbled down, but I regained my balance and kept the book firmly clasped in my hands. I could not lose it.

When I made it back to my room, it was empty, of course. I locked the door behind me and dove into my bed, feeling much safer with the covers wrapped around me. My heart had been pounding the whole way to my door and I must have glanced over my shoulder at least 20 times. My paranoia had stuck with me after I was out of the library causing me to imagine the sound of footsteps following me here. Each time I looked around me, I was greeted by an empty hallway. No one else was there, with the exception of a guard every now and again. Still, only now did I feel fully safe. I glanced at the clock on the wall. It was only 9:45 p.m. My roommates would be at the party for at least another hour. Ava never liked to be the first to leave an event. I was thankful to have alone time to read the book without the girls breathing down my neck, asking a million questions.

I flipped past the first few pages and came to a table of contents. It showed chapters with names I didn't recognize at first. Alice Adams. Florence Haggen. Constance Patterson. I made it halfway down the page and my eyes froze, fixating on two words: *"Fallen Angel"* was scrawled on the thin paper. The words became blurry and difficult to read, and I realized my hands were trembling. I put the book down and took a few calming breaths before picking it back up to look at the page number. *Page 103.*

I quickly flipped through the book. Again, there on the top of the page, were the words. *"Fallen Angel."* Well, this is what I wanted to know, right? No sense in chickening out now. I started to read.

In the beginning of time there was only one being. This being stood for all good. This being created trees, oceans, animals, and even new beings to cure his loneliness. He wished for a family. So, the being created two sons and two daughters. These five lived on a desolate island in perfect harmony. There was no hurt. No pain. No jealousy or rage.

But nature became unbalanced. There could not only be good in the world. Where there is peace there must also be wickedness. So, nature corrected this mistake. Rage began to slowly overtake one of the being's sons. He tried to hide it, to suppress it. After all, such feelings were unknown to his family. The son watched the way his father controlled everything surrounding them. The son wanted to do the same. He wanted to create. He wanted to be powerful. But not only powerful. _More_ powerful than his siblings. More powerful than his father.

Each sibling had powers, much like their father only dulled. It was as if their father had taken his powers and spread them out amongst the children. None of them possessed his strength. They would never be as he was.

As time went on the children became aware of their aging. They watched in horror as wrinkles developed on their skin where there had previously been none. Their bodies ached where they never had before. The son looked at his father and saw he had no wrinkles. He had no aches. He was riddled with even more jealousy.

The son felt his magic coursing through his blood, leading him to what he already sensed. He knew in his heart if he were to murder his siblings, he would steal their youth. He would lose his siblings forever but gain life in return. The secret contempt he felt for his father made the choice simple. He created a spell to take the lives of his siblings and began with his sisters. The son snuck into their tent late one night when their father was far away. He took their life quickly, using his spell, and after their heart beat their last beats, he felt their youth. When the father returned, he was saddened and confused by their deaths. There had never been hurt in their family. There had never been loss. So, the father grieved, but never suspected his own son.

When seven nights had passed and the moon was full in the sky, the son took the life of his only brother. He felt youth coursing through his veins, as expected. But now he could see there was an unexpected effect. Overtaking his brother had been easier than anticipated. The son realized when he killed his siblings, he not only took their youth, but also their power. He watched his father cry with pity. His father was weak to allow love to blind him. His father grew lonely again and created more family, many more this time. More than the son could keep count of. The son was enraged by his father's power. He became more jealous, angrier.

When the day came that he saw a new wrinkle, he knew what he must do. He took the lives of more siblings. This time he knew he could not stop. He felt their youth and power. He could not control his rage. His father watched more and more of his children disappear and soon realized the dark truth. His eldest son had not aged in quite some time and his body had become disfigured. His son did not look like the rest of his siblings. His skin was harder, rougher. His forehead was larger and his muscles more prominent. Two small antlers had begun to pierce through his head as if he were becoming like the animals around him. His father knew this was not right. He knew this was a danger to all.

The father confronted his eldest son. The son knew his father could destroy him, despite all of the power he had acquired over time but saw he would not. His love was too strong. It blinded him again. Weakened him. The son knew he must act then. If he could defeat his father, he would have true immortality. He would become ruler of the earth. He would have his father's power. The son could see everything he longed for right in front of him. He took his chance, spelling his father again and again, feeling no remorse. His father did not fight back and began to weaken as his son slowly stole his power. The father did not have much time left. If he did not act now, he would not survive. But he could not take the life of his son.

The father stood with tears in his eyes and, using every ounce of magic he had left, banished his son to the Underworld.

The father rested for quite some time. He was weakened, but his other children cared for him, nursing him back to health until he was nearly as powerful as he was at the beginning of time. The father waited patiently, but his powers never fully returned.

His son was alive. He had not taken his life, but he was banished to the Underworld, unable to return to his home. He was cold and lonely at first. He felt rage towards his father for banishing him from the one home he had ever known. However, he soon found that he was more powerful than he had ever been on Earth. Much more powerful. He could feel it coursing through every inch of his being. He had what he wanted. Finally. Power and youth. All he needed was a kingdom to rule. And soon he would have one.

I flipped the pages again and again longing for more of the story but finding nothing but new stories. I had answers but felt desperate to know more. A strange feeling overcame me. This longing for more and more reminded me of the story of the Fallen Angel. So, I slammed the book shut and placed it on my nightstand. I knew enough. More than I even expected to.

I knew that Mary Langley had gotten her soul stealing spell from the Fallen Angel himself. I knew that killing another witch with this spell stole their youth, as well as their powers.

I knew how the Fallen Angel came to be, a story our school obviously didn't like to advertise. And I knew that the Fallen Angel had been like us at one time. A witch with an average amount of powers. A witch who aged like the rest of us. But using his spell he changed and became nearly as powerful as the Divinity. If the Fallen Angel could do this, if Mary Langley could use the same spell for the same purpose, could this happen again? Is that what was happening at North End this very moment?

8
LEVEL·HEADED

I was startled awake by someone shaking my shoulders. I peeled them open to see Lillian standing over me fully dressed. Had she just made it back from the party? What time was it?

"Are you okay?" Lillian asked, clearly concerned.

"Yes," I answered, confused. I sat up to see Ava and Daliah sitting at the end of my bed. Their faces were worried, too.

"You were asleep...for a really long time," Lillian said slowly. I looked at the clock on the well. Three o'clock? In the afternoon? "And you're covered in sweat. We tried to wake you up a few times before..." Her voice trailed off and three sets of eyes waited for me to reply. I assessed myself before answering. I felt my head and was surprised to find Lillian was right. It was sticky with sweat. I sat up slowly, expecting to feel nauseous or dizzy. Maybe I had a virus or something. But when I sat up, I felt fine. Well rested. Normal.

"I feel fine," I said.

"Are you sure?" Daliah asked, doubtful. "We were about to call a nurse."

"Yes. Really. I'm not sure why I slept so long, but...I feel fine," I reassured them. It didn't take much reassurance before Ava and Daliah were off doing their own thing again, but it took longer to convince Lillian. She asked several more times that day.

"Are you sure you don't want to go get checked out in the hospital wing?" she asked once more as she laid down for bed. I was gazing out our window at the moon brightening up the sky. It was less than a week until All Hallow's Eve and the full moon.

"I'm fine, I promise," I said for a final time. It was difficult to say much more to reassure her when I wasn't sure what had happened myself. I didn't even remember falling asleep the night before. But the day had come and gone, and Lillian had waited and waited for something to be off with me. It never happened. I went about the day like any other Sunday.

"Well, wake me up if you feel sick or something," Lillian said before turning off her lamp and pulling the covers up to her chin. I still hadn't told her what I read in the book. Maybe a part of me was scared to explain it. I didn't want the book to have anything to do with my extended slumber, so I didn't say a word. If I didn't speak it, then it couldn't be true, right?

I closed the curtains and sat on my bed. I wasn't exactly tired yet, so I laid there for a while going over the day and trying my best to remember falling asleep last night, but I kept coming up blank. Eventually, I gave up. *Oh well,* I thought. *At least I got a good night's rest.* I shut my eyes and thought of happier things to help me sleep. Like Miles' eyes or Lillian's laugh or my parent's dinner parties. My head was filled with these beautiful images as my body began drifting. I felt calm and relaxed. So, I was unsure why the last images in my mind were horns on a figure with rough skin.

* * *

"Josie?" I heard Professor Rose's voice over the chatter and shuffling. The extra study hall I had signed up for had just ended, and most people were making their way out of the room. When I looked up, she was motioning me to come to her desk at the front of the room. My heart rate picked up slightly. *Why is she asking me to stay after class?* I turned to look at Lillian, who was waiting for me by the door. She raised her eyebrow and I shrugged lightly. She stepped outside with her books, but I had no doubt she would be waiting for me in the garden.

My mind immediately went to the worst scenario possible. I prayed she wasn't having me stay back because I was in trouble. Or, even worse, because my grades were suffering. I thoroughly enjoyed her class, and if my grades were bad enough to stay after, I would be completely humiliated.

I made my way to Rose's desk, wringing my hands, as the room cleared out. "How are you, dear?" she asked when the class was empty. She was smiling warmly, which made me feel a little less uneasy. Surely I wasn't in trouble if she was smiling at me.

"I'm fine," I smiled back. "How are you, Professor Rose?"

"Oh, I am well. Thank you for asking." She twirled her fingers for a moment like she was unsure of what to say next. "I hope you don't find this...inappropriate, but I have a gift for you." She walked back to her closet by her desk and pulled something out. It was covered in silk, but I could tell it was some sort of clothing. It was on a hanger and was nearly as tall as Professor Rose. It looked like...a dress.

She lifted the material up and laid it on her massive desk. It didn't even cover half of the length of the table. "You looked so beautiful in this, Josie. I know your mother would want you to have it," she said as she lifted up the satin, revealing the gorgeous black dress she saw me trying on this weekend.

I gasped. "Professor Rose...I-I..." I was absolutely

speechless.

"Now, before you say anything about the expense, know that I have more than enough wealth for myself. I have no children of my own, you know," her voice trembled just a bit when she said the word children, and I suddenly realized how little I knew of Rose's past. Had she tried to have children at some point? Had they passed away? I looked up to see tears in her eyes and a lump formed in my throat. "I want it to be a special night. One to remember." She smiled and we both choked back tears.

I ran my hand along the bottom of the dress, appreciating each sparkle. "This is the most incredible gift...Thank you, Professor Rose," I said simply.

"You're welcome, dear. Now be on your way. I want you to take this straight to your room. I will write you a late excuse for your next class." She grabbed a pen and a notecard and scribbled down a few words that would easily excuse my tardiness. When other professors saw Rose's name on something, they did not question it. She handed me the note and, after covering the dress up again, the hanger. I took them both, smiling, and met Lillian outside the classroom.

* * *

The first three days of the week had been blissful for me. I got my dream dress from my most admired professor, and I was spending all my free time with Miles and Lillian. Life could not have been better. Which is why I felt guilty the majority of the time. Around every corner, I was met by a tall, muscular guard that reminded of why they were here in the first place. Laura was still gone. She would never get to attend a Hallow's Eve ball or laugh with her best friend or kiss the perfect guy. It didn't seem fair that I was having all of these good days while her friends were missing her. I started spending more time learning about the Divinity. Maybe I was searching for answers I would never find, but some witches, like Professor Rose, found comfort in praying to him.

So, I had been giving it a try. Each night, for the past three nights, I prayed to him. I prayed for Laura's family and friends. I prayed for protection for the school. I prayed that I would feel less guilty about enjoying my life to the fullest. I even tried praying for my dad one night, but the picture of him sitting in his chair alone sent a pain through my chest that was strong enough to stop me in the middle of my sentence. I wasn't sure if it was actually helping or if it was more of a placebo effect, but as I got ready for my date with Miles on Wednesday night, I only felt excitement. As I walked down the halls, I made sure to divert my eyes every time I saw a guard. I hadn't felt guilty yet, but there was no need to push it. I locked my eyes straight ahead the whole time.

I met Miles in front of the main entrance of the school. As I walked down the spiral stairs, I peeked down at him by the door with each rotation. He stood, almost a head above everyone else in the lobby. His dark, curly hair was tied back away from his face tonight. I had never seen him without it being free to fall wherever, and I felt a pang in my heart. I was suddenly terribly nervous. With each rotation around the spirals I noticed something new about him. The first thing I saw was his hair, and I wondered what I would tangle my hands in later if it stayed pin back. Then I noticed his blue sweater and thought of how perfectly it would match his blue eyes. I wondered if he wore it on purpose as I flashed back to the time I had mentioned how the color looked great on him. That was a few weeks before he asked me out. I wondered if he remembered. Finally, I noticed his dark jeans with his hand stuffed into the pockets.

By the time I reached the bottom of the stairs he was pacing back and forth between the students passing by. If I didn't know better, I would have guessed he was nervous too, which seemed very unlike him.

As I approached him, I was struck with the realization that it may not always be this way. If we continued seeing each other, we would become more comfortable or eventually maybe even grow apart. There might not always be this electricity in the air and my heart might not always double its beating when his lips met mine. So, I paused in the middle of the walkway to enjoy this moment and take every piece of him in. This was a glorious feeling, one I would remember for the rest of my life.

As much as I loved watching him when he didn't think anyone was looking, I knew I couldn't stand another minute without his hand in mine. I ached to touch him even though we had spoken just last night. A full day without seeing him was much too long. I took long strides to close the gap between us. He turned to see me coming and his face lit up along with his eyes. *Blue*, I smiled. I reached my hand out and his fingers filled the spaces between mine. I sighed with relief.

He pulled me in for a hug and buried his face in my hair. "Hey, you," he whispered.

"Hey," I said as I pulled away to look at his face again. "I missed you." Normally I would have been too nervous to tell him such a thing, but tonight I felt braver than I ever had. I knew I couldn't let these moments pass us by without telling him how I felt. Of course, I held back a little. I could have told him that his face had not left my mind since we parted yesterday or that even my dreams were filled with him and his easy smile, but I thought a simple "I miss you" would suffice for now. I didn't want to scare him away.

"I missed you, too. You look cozy." I had on a turtleneck sweater that was two sizes too big for me but kept me very warm. Plus, it reminded me of my dad. It was one of the only things I had that reminded me of him without bringing too much pain. "Which is perfect. I was thinking we could walk down the trail to the ocean."

I hesitated, thinking of walking alone in the black night. Normally, I would love just the thought of being outside at night with the moon shining bright above us, but things were different now. "Are you sure that's a good idea? With everything that's been going on?" I asked, nervously.

"Well, they have guards on the outside of the castle, too, so I figured we'd be just as safe out there as we would be in here," he shrugged, but changed his tone when he noticed my hesitance. "Unless you don't feel comfortable. We could do something el--"

"I think a walk sounds nice. Plus, if there are guards around then what's the harm?" He smiled, relieved.

"Let's go, then," he held out his arm and I looped mine through it. "You'll love this view. It's even better than the one we saw in the stairwell." We headed out the front entrance and the cool breeze almost took my breath away. The temperature had dropped drastically since this morning on the balcony. I snuggled up to Miles' arm to keep me warm.

We crossed the bridge and headed down the trail that was just to the left of the school, and I saw that Miles was right. There were guards outside the school. It was a funny thing now that, despite my hesitation, I felt even safer outside in the open air than I had inside. A cool, fall night was my favorite kind. The stars were twinkling above, and the moon was reflecting on the ocean. The trail was short, and I could already see the waves and smell the ocean air.

There was no actual beach on the island. When you made it to any of the edges, you were met with a steep drop, leading straight down to crashing waves. So, we stopped a short distance from the cliff. The grass around us was tall and thin, and it swayed along with the breeze. I had never been down this trail before and was in awe of the view. The sound of the waves was peaceful, and I squinted my eyes as if I could see where the ocean ended if I looked hard enough, even though that was impossible. It seemed to go on forever.

Miles sat down in the grass and patted his lap. I crawled on it and wrapped my arms around his neck, pressing my cheek against his as we both took in the view. We were quiet for a long time, just listening to the ocean. Miles broke the silence first.

"Josie," he said, followed by an audible gulp. I peeled my eyes away from the ocean to gaze at Miles. "I'm really glad I have you." I smiled and looked down feeling a pitter in my heart. "I haven't had much of a family these past few years and I haven't been close to many people...well...basically my whole life. It always kind of felt like something was missing. I thought it was because my mom left or because my dad and I have grown apart, but now I know that it was *you* that was missing. You're already such a big part of my life. Like a puzzle piece that fit perfectly. It seems crazy, but I can't imagine my life without you in it now." My heart swelled because his words were the same thing I had been thinking these past couple of weeks. I pressed my lips against his for a moment.

"You know I feel the same way, right?" I asked, simply, knowing I would never be able to put it as eloquently as he had.

"I'm in love with you, Josie," he whispered and I nearly gasped.

I hadn't expected him to say *that*, but when the words left his mouth, I had no doubt I returned the feeling. A smile broke across my face so wide that my cheeks hurt. I giggled and once I started, I couldn't stop. I was high on life and on this moment and elation filled my whole body from head to toe. Things had never been so perfect. I kissed both of his cheeks in between my giggling and finally said, "I'm in love with you, too."

Now I wasn't the only one giggling. Miles couldn't help himself and I wondered if his heart felt as whole as mine did in this moment. "You do?" he laughed.

"Yes," I nodded. He rose to his feet with me cradled in his arms and spun me around. He placed me down on my feet and we kissed and laughed so loudly I was sure the guards outside would hear us. "We're insane!" I exclaimed.

"Yeah, but at least we're insane together." Our laughter finally started to fade as I wrapped my arms around his neck and he wrapped his around my waist, pulling me closer. I wasn't sure how long we stood out there by the water. All I knew is his lips didn't leave mine the whole time.

* * *

When I got back from my date with Miles, I was on cloud nine. My heart was full. I had no doubts about my feelings for him, but I also couldn't wait to see what Lillian's reaction would be. Would she think I was insane? A lovesick puppy? Probably. We had only been together for a short time, which, I have to admit, *does* sound crazy. But what was that saying Mom used to use? *When you know, you know.* That's it. That's what it had been like for her and Dad. People thought they were rushing when they got engaged after only six months of dating, but they were the happiest couple I had ever seen. None of my friends' parents held a candle to what they had. Plus, Miles has been my friend for a while, too. For months! *See?* I thought to myself, already preparing my argument in case Lillian disapproved. *Maybe I'm not as crazy as I seem.* Even if I was, I didn't care.

I finally made it back to the room after practicing how to

tell Lillian the whole walk there. If I was a crazy, hopeless romantic, then Lillian was a level-headed doubter. I couldn't blame her for using rationality when it came to relationships. Even though her family was very close, her parents had divorced when she was younger, and her mother drilled it into her head that marriage was a crazy thing that only led to heartbreak. Not the greatest thing to tell a kid when they're a mere 10 years old, but who am I to judge? Now, Lillian didn't believe *that,* but I doubt she would believe I should be saying "love" after such a short time.

I took a deep breath and swung open the door, expecting to see Lillian waiting for me on her bed. But instead I saw an empty room. I glanced towards her closet to see if she was inside searching for some piece of clothing, but she wasn't there either. Her lamp near her bed was still on, the only light in the room. She must have gone to the bathroom. She hadn't mentioned having any plans for the night. I guess she could have plans without telling me, but that would be a first. She must just be in the bathroom. I laid in my bed and stared at the ceiling, basking in the high I was still on. I replayed the night in my head while I waited: Miles' eyes burning through mine. The way his voice sounded when he whispered my name. The way his lips felt pressed against mine. The way his hands shaped my waist.

* * *

I sat up in my bed and let out a whimper. *Did I fall asleep?* I was still fully clothed and on top of my sheet. *I guess so.* I looked over at Lillian's bed and saw that it was empty. Her lamp was still the only light in the room. I peered over to the other corner and saw two lumps in my roommates' beds. They were there, asleep, but Lillian wasn't. I looked at the clock, still not feeling too worried. Then, I saw the time read 1:38. In the morning. *Where is she?* Panic started creeping in.

I reached for my cell phone. The screen only showed the time. No missed phone calls. No texts. I dialed Lillian's number. *Ring. Ring. Ring. Ring. Ring.* Nothing. I tried again. Nothing. The third time I tried it went straight to voicemail. Weird. Why would it ring the first two times, then go straight to voicemail? Unless she was ignoring me. Why would she do that though? Was she mad at me? Or in trouble? My paranoia felt out of control.

Even if it was the latter, there was nothing I could do. I had no idea where she could even be. The castle is huge. I wouldn't be able to search for it tonight. I decided to call campus security. They answered on the second ring, obviously not busy with some crisis involving Lillian, which made me feel better right away.

"Hello?" grumbled a deep voice.

"Hi," I whispered trying not to wake Ava and Daliah. "Um...my roommate has not made it back to our room yet, and I'm getting a little worried. She usually tells me where she's going, and she won't answer her phone and it's really late-" I realized I was rambling so I paused to see what he would say.

"What is your roommate's name?" he asked in a monotone voice.

"Lillian Bishop," I answered promptly.

"We haven't heard anything about any Lillians tonight. You sure she's not just staying in a friend's room?" He sounded bored.

"Well, she would tell me if she was staying somewhere else. It's really strange that I haven't heard from her..." I trailed off. He did not seem as concerned as me.

"Honestly, kid, we've been getting several calls a night like this. A roommate doesn't come home right away, and kids panic because the...uh, well...recent events, but it always turns out that their roommate is just staying at a friend's place or out causing trouble. They're never in danger."

"Could you at least look around for her or something?" I suddenly felt silly even though I knew my feelings of concern were justified. Lillian wouldn't be out causing trouble at 1:38 am.

"I'll take her name down, but we have guys all over the school. If something was wrong, they'd most likely catch it."

That was true. They *did* have guards all over the castle. I saw them every day. "What's your name, kid?"

"Josie," I said simply.

"If I hear anything, I'll call you, okay?" he grumbled.

"I--" He hung up the phone before I could say anything else. I thought about what he said. There were guards all over the castle. He hadn't heard any bad news all night. Most people were overreacting. I repeated those things in my head until I drifted back to sleep with a sick feeling in my chest.

9
LOSING MY FAMILY

I could feel the bags under my eyes as soon as I opened them. My dreams had turned to nightmares halfway through the night, but they were foggy. I couldn't remember what they were about. I stretched and looked at the clock on the wall. It was five minutes before my alarm would go off. I decided to close my eyes and enjoy these last few minutes of peace, snuggled under my blankets before I started the day. I flipped onto my side, facing Lillian's bed. Suddenly the terrible images in my head from last night came flooding back, crystal clear. I realized only half of them were nightmares.

Lillian's bed was still empty. She had never come home. All night I dreamt of her being attacked or laying on the floor crumpled like a wad of paper. Like Laura. My heart started pounding and I could feel cold sweat forming on my forehead.

168

I reached for my phone to see if I had any missed calls. Nothing. No calls from Lillian or the security guard. Not even a "good morning" text from Miles. *What is going on with everyone?*

I hopped out of bed and walked over to Daliah's bed to shake her awake. "Huh?" she mumbled as she reluctantly opened her eyes.

"Were you two with Lillian last night? Have you heard from her?" I asked urgently.

"No," Daliah yawned and stretched, obviously not picking up on my tone. "I haven't seen her since yesterday evening. Why?"

"She didn't come back to our room last night," I said. This widened her eyes a little and she finally sat up.

"She's probably with that dude from the party," Ava mumbled from her bed. The covers were still over her head.

"Oh yeah! He was totally flirting with her, wasn't he?" Daliah giggled, no longer worried.

"What dude?" I scoffed. Lillian hadn't mentioned meeting anyone.

"Just some older boy. He wanted to hang out with her, so she probably just stayed the night at his place," Ava mumbled.

Daliah raised her eyebrows and said, "Go Lillian!"

"Can you please shut up now so I can enjoy these last few minutes of sleep?" Ava grumbled. Daliah obliged and laid back down on her pillow. I was left alone in the silence, knowing

Lillian would never go over to some random boy's room and stay the night. I could see these two wouldn't be any help. Ava was already snoring again.

Relaxing was no longer an option for me, so I walked to my dresser, grabbed my bathroom bag, and headed down the hall, hoping I could investigate while I got ready for the day. Several girls were already in the bathroom doing their makeup or showering. I asked each and every one if they had seen Lillian this morning or last night. None of them had. That's when it really hit me. Hard. Something bad happened. I could feel it in the pit of my stomach. A wave of nausea washed over me and I almost ran to the toilet to throw up, but I held it together long enough to get to the shower.

When the water started pouring, so did my tears. It may have been irrational and pointless—my tears couldn't solve anything—and I couldn't even explain why I was crying, but I could not stop myself. My mind wouldn't slow down long enough to take stock of the situation. Maybe if it would, I could make sense of everything. All I knew was that if something happened to Lillian, I would have already gotten a phone call from that guard, right? They would notify her roommates right away. But alone in the shower, I went to the worst-case scenario. The gnawing thought of living each morning without her in the bed next to me was enough to send me into hysterics.

I stood under the water until my tears stopped. I hadn't even bothered to take a proper shower; I only stood under the water for an unknown amount of time. If she was in that room when I got back, I would be seriously pissed.

I didn't bother drying my hair or putting on makeup. I went straight back to the room. It was empty. I grabbed my phone and called the guard again. No answer. I tried three more times before I gave up and decided to take matters into my own hands. I threw my damp hair in a bun and tossed on some random clothes, not even bothering to see if they matched. I grabbed my school bag and headed out the door.

* * *

I spent the hour before class walking and walking and walking. When it was time for Professor Rose's class to begin I was on the opposite side of campus, so I skipped it completely, continuing my search instead. I covered at least half of the campus, but there was no sign of Lillian. I even asked random students if they had seen a petite redhead. No one had. Confused and answerless, I scuffled to class alone and sat in the back row so I wouldn't draw attention to myself if I got a phone call or message and had to make an exit.

Usually, I don't bring my phone with me to classes. I hardly ever used it at all, but today I packed it in my bag and made sure I could hear it vibrate. Class had just started when I heard its buzz, alerting me to a text message. I scooped it out of my bag, hoping to see Lillian's name on the screen, but it was from Miles. I opened it immediately, even though we weren't supposed to text in class. I could not have cared less at the moment. "Come to the hospital wing ASAP. Lillian is here." My heart jumped to my throat. Lillian is *there*? What did that mean? I typed back, "Is she okay?"

The reply was so immediate I wasn't sure how he even had time to type it. "Not sure. Just come." The phone fell out of my hand and clattered on the floor. A few students in the next row up turned to look at me, but the professor didn't seem to notice. He continued rambling. My brain was in a haze, but I knew I had to leave. I picked up my phone, shoved it in my bag, and thanked my lucky stars I had chosen to sit so close to the back of the room. I slipped my bag over my shoulder and tiptoed out. I didn't stop to make sure the door closed gently, so the wind ended up slamming it closed with a huge bang. *Oh well.* I was already gone anyway, and my feet were not going to stop for anything.

The hospital ward was a good five-minute walk from where I was, and before I knew it, I was running. I shoved bad thoughts out of my mind. I couldn't think the worst. I couldn't picture Lillian crumbling on the floor like Laura...*No!* No, that did not happen. She must just be sick with a virus or something. I would get there and she would laugh because I would be covered in sweat from running the whole way for no reason. She would be back in our room by nightfall.

My emotions were all over the place and suddenly I was overcome with rage. Why would Miles be so vague in his text? It was just cruel. And how did he know where she was before me? Why am I out of the loop? Someone from the medical team should have gotten a hold of me first. I was her roommate and best friend, after all.

I reached the door to the medical wing faster than I thought I would, but when I felt a bead of sweat drip from my forehead, I realized why I arrived so quickly. I was gasping trying to catch my breath. I wasn't in the best shape, and the panic rising in my chest certainly didn't make breathing any easier. I tried to catch my breath before opening the door, but as my breathing slowed the adrenaline wore off and my legs started to throb. *Forget it*, I thought. Who cares if they think I'm crazy? I shoved the door open and was greeted by a receptionist.

"Good morning, dear. How may I help you?" She was an older lady with yellow, puffy hair. I remembered her from when I got the flu last year.

"Hi, I'm looking for Lillian Bish-" I was interrupted by a familiar voice.

"Josie! She's back here!" Miles appeared out of the door

that led to the hospital rooms. "This is her roommate, Josie, the one I said to look out for," he addressed the lady at the front desk.

"Oh, yes. Go on back, dear." She looked at me with a tight, forced smile. Miles took my hand in his and led me through the door and down the hallway. The walls were white, and the lights were bright. Too bright. It was uncomfortable and I had to squint like I just stepped outside on the sunniest day of the year. It was so different from the rest of the castle. This couldn't be a relaxing environment for sick people.

"How is she? What happened?" I demanded as he dragged me down the hall, not quite sprinting, but definitely not walking. We stopped in front of the last room on the left. He turned to face me and put his hands on my arms, gently.

"She's in a coma, Josie. They're not sure what happened, but she has severe injuries," Miles said, cutting straight to the point. I appreciated his lack of sugar coating since there was obviously no time for that, but it made my head feel all swimmy. My knees started buckling beneath me, and Miles wrapped his arms around me before I collapsed on the floor. It occurred to me that my full weight was in his arms, but I couldn't make myself stand on my own.

He started whispering in my ear in an attempt to calm me down. "They think she's going to come out of it. It seems like someone tried to cast a spell to harm her, but they must not have done it properly. They can heal her, Josie. They will heal her." His reassurances helped. Where there was a spell to harm, there was usually a spell to heal. I could partially feel my legs again. Enough to stand on my own, but Miles kept his arms around me protectively just in case. I was furious again.

"What do you mean magic? What happened? Who used magic on her?" My words spilled out uncontrollably. I tried to shove past Miles to get into the room where they were keeping her, but he stopped me.

"Josie, look at me," he whispered gently, pulling back to look me in the eyes. "It's okay. She will be okay. Right now, it looks worse than what it is."

"Who did this?" I yelled, already fearing the worst. She was in a coma from a spell gone wrong. Someone obviously wanted to hurt her. Maybe even *kill* her. "Was it the same person who…" I couldn't finish the sentence, but I didn't have to. Miles knew what I was thinking. Because he was thinking the same thing.

"We can't be sure of that. The spell seems very similar, but the witch who did it this time doesn't seem experienced or perhaps they were preoccupied. They messed up and it saved her life." I put my hands over my face and broke free of his arms. I paced the hall with my eyes covered by my hands and started sobbing again. Just the thought of Lillian being gone, taken away from me, from the world was enough to send me into hysterics. That was nearly my reality. I ran back to Miles' arms. "I need her," I murmured, my voice cracking. I had never meant something so much in my life. I've already lost the most important member of my family. My mother. I couldn't afford to lose another.

"She's going to be okay, Josie," he reassured me again, clutching me to his chest. "Do you want to see her?" he asked when my tears slowed. I nodded. "Remember, it's not as bad as it looks. They just have her hooked up to a lot of monitors to track her healing." He cracked the door open for me, and I stepped into the room.

Thankfully, this room was not as bright as the hallway. The lights were dimmed, but I could still see the damage. Lillian had bruises on her cheeks and collarbone. Her wrist was wrapped in a large, white bandage. Her eyes were closed, but she didn't look peaceful. She was connected to machines. I didn't bother to count how many. I knew one of them was tracking her heartbeat because I could hear the beeping, but I couldn't tell what the others were for. *Miles warned me it looked worse than what it really was*, I reminded myself. But it looked bad. Really bad.

Miles came up from behind me and hugged me from behind. He kissed me quickly, leaving a wet spot on my cheek. "I just saw her yesterday. She was fine. She could have died," my voice shook on that last part.

"She didn't though. I know it doesn't seem like it, but she got lucky," Miles said with his arms still wrapped around me. I clung to them.

"She's my family," I whispered. "I can't lose her."

"Well, it's a good thing you're not going to!" he said cheerfully. He was really trying to make me feel better. Just then a nurse peeped her head through the door.

"Knock knock." She walked in with a smile on her face, checked a couple of monitors, then turned to face us. She explained how Lillian was doing, using a lot of complicated terms I had never heard before. I didn't ask questions. I just let her give her spiel. By the end of her speech I was confused, but slightly relieved. The nurse thought Lillian would recover, too. She was as optimistic as Miles.

I skipped my last class of the day and stayed in Lillian's room. There was a TV, so I watched old American game shows for a while. Eventually I got tired of hearing the audience laugh track and broke out my textbooks. Since I skipped my last class and left one early, I was due for some studying. Before I knew it, the clock by Lillian's bed read 7 p.m. I had been here for six hours already. I looked over at Lillian. She still didn't look peaceful, and I felt guilty knowing I had to leave. But the grumble of my stomach forced me out of my seat. The café closed in less than an hour, so I had to eat something before it was too late. I told Lillian I would be back later just in case she could hear me. I signed the "sign out" sheet quickly before darting to the café.

I grabbed something to go before heading back to my room. By the time I finished my food, visiting hours at the medical ward were over. I spent the rest of the night watching old movies on Lillian's laptop. I sent Miles a few messages, but he was busy with homework and I didn't want to keep bugging him. I had a few other friends I could have hung out with to take my mind off everything, but I wasn't in the mood. It felt wrong that I was here capable of hanging out with friends while Lillian was all alone in a hospital bed unable to even open her eyes. Eventually, I drifted to sleep, unsure of the time, wrapped in a blanket on Lillian's bed with her laptop still playing old movies.

* * *

The laptop must have died at some point because I woke up in the middle of the night and the screen was black. An uneasy feeling washed over me until I looked over at the other beds to see my roommates, with the exception of Lillian of course, were asleep. I felt more at ease since they were here, and I wasn't alone. I closed the laptop and scooted over to my bed, keeping the cover wrapped around me. I laid on my side and faced the door. A crevice of light from the hallway was peeking through the bottom of it. I pictured footsteps approaching the door and standing in front of the light. I pictured Lillian sneaking in late and crawling into bed. I started to drift off while I was imagining these images until they seemed real. Almost too real. I could have sworn I actually saw feet outside my door as my eyes slid close.

10

HALLOW'S EVE

I woke up an hour before my alarm went off and knew I had fallen asleep early because I felt well-rested, despite the dreams of footsteps in the hall. I was thankful to feel re-energized because I wanted to see Lillian before my first class. I got ready quickly, rushing through the shower, and didn't bother with any makeup. There was no one else in the café, so I quickly grabbed a piece of toast and some bacon before heading to the medical ward. I snatched Lillian's favorite muffin, too, because if by some miracle she was awake, she would appreciate a blueberry muffin. It was probably silly to hope I would walk into her room and see her sitting up in bed smiling, but I had to think positively if I wanted to make it through this day without tears.

My hopes were shoved back at me when I reached her

room. It was dead silent. Only a few overnight nurses lingered in the halls. No one else was even visiting at this time. There were only three other patients in the ward, and it sounded like they were all sleeping. I plopped down in the same wooden chair beside the bed that I sat in yesterday. It creaked when I sat, and the sound seemed to echo in the noiseless room. The only sound for the next hour was my chewing and the nurses' tennis shoes squeaking on the linoleum as they walked by the room.

I checked the clock on the wall. I knew I needed to leave for class sooner than later, so I placed the blueberry muffin on a napkin on the nightstand and threw away my leftover food. When I passed the receptionist, she smiled at me warmly. She was obviously just starting her shift because she looked well-rested unlike the nurses who were finishing their shifts down the hall, running on fumes. I walked past the desk and she told me goodbye. When I looked down to say goodbye to her as well, my eyes were drawn to the sign-in sheet on her desk. I had forgotten to sign in that morning. *Oops.* I scribbled my name on the "sign-in" side of the paper, but when I went to write it down on the "sign out" section I noticed something peculiar. There were only two names following my signature from last night.

Josie Parker

Miles Preston

Frances Barns

Frances? I paused mid-motion to stare at the names. *Who was Frances visiting last night?* There were only three other patients besides Lillian, and I had never seen Frances with any of them. They definitely weren't friends of hers. In fact, it would be odd if she even knew the other patients at all.

"Are you alright, dear?" the woman at the desk asked. I realized I was still holding the pen in midair and had yet to sign my name.

"Oh, yeah. Sorry." I scribbled it down and quickly exited the room.

"Have a good day," she called as the door swung close. I didn't respond. The further I walked, the more confused I became. Surely Frances wasn't there to see Lillian. Was she? But then again, it didn't make sense for her to visit any of the other patients. It had to be Lillian.

The more I thought of Frances having the nerve to visit Lillian when all she had ever done was treat her like dirt for years, the angrier I became. *She has no right to walk into that room. Lillian would have cursed her out if she was conscious!* I thought, covering more ground with each stride. Luckily, I was on my way to the class I had with her. I would confront her as soon as I walked in the room. My anger was giving me courage.

I was rounding the corner to the classroom, moving full steam ahead when a realization stopped me in my tracks. *Miles was there before me yesterday,* I thought. He left shortly after I arrived. *Then, why is his name after mine on the sign out sheet?* A girl who was walking too closely behind me slammed into my back, distracting me from my thoughts. I almost toppled over with her on top of me. We both steadied ourselves and she gave me a scowl, as she continued walking.

"Sorry," I said sarcastically. Her scowl only added fire to the flame burning in my chest. Now, I was uncontrollably furious. I half-ran, half-stomped to the classroom door. I barged inside, causing the door to fling open too hard and hit the wall. It made a loud *bang* and several students jerked their heads to the back of the room, searching for the cause of the sound. Their eyes landed on me. I didn't care. I headed straight for Frances who was, of course, in the first row. Several sets of eyes followed me. I was glad. *Good. Let's give them a show, then.* This was a long time coming.

Frances saw me barreling towards her with my arms swinging wildly by my sides. Her expression changed from its usual smugness to confusion. "Who the hell were you visiting in the medical wing?" I demanded before I even made it all the way to her. Her eyes flickered to what I thought was worry, then went quickly back to stone.

"What in the Underworld are you referring to?" Frances stood, delicately placed her hand on her chest and gave the people around her a confused look as she spoke, as if I was a mad woman. I was. They were all staring at me, but for once, I didn't care.

"I saw your name on the sign-in sheet, Frances. Right under mine from last night. So, who was it? Lillian." It came out as more of a statement than a question.

I could clearly see the anxiety in her face this time, but she fought hard to hide it. "I-I…" she stuttered. This was the first time I had ever seen Frances without a witty retort, so I took advantage.

"So, it *was* her?" I had my answer. "How *dare* you? Why were you there? You hate her so there must be some diabolical reason for your visit." My words were spilling out so quickly I wondered if she could even understand all of them.

"Did you ever consider that I might be concerned for the girl?" her voice was calm, sweet, and quiet while an innocent look was painted on her face.

"That's a load of bull--"

"Ms. Parker," a stern voice echoed through the room. I heard the heels hitting the floor and knew who it was before I dared to turn and look. Headmistress Craw had arrived to class.

That explained the innocent look smeared on Frances' face. I twisted my head over my shoulder to see Craw heading straight for me. When I glanced back at Frances, she wore her regular smug smile. She sat down before Craw made it to me. I whipped around to face her. "See me after class, please," Craw whispered.

"Yes, ma'am," I responded as politely as I could muster. My blood was still boiling from the confrontation, and I hardly cared that Craw caught me. I took my seat a few rows back, waiting silently for class to begin. That was the first time I'd ever seen Frances falter since I met her. She looked worried, even if it was just for a moment. She even stuttered. I knew something was wrong with her visiting the medical ward and that conversation proved it. But I still didn't have the answer I needed. *Why?*

Headmistress Craw started class, but I couldn't stay focused and gave up on trying to listen to the lesson. Since I had time to cool down, my mind wandered back to Miles. His name was right below Frances'. I still had no answers for that either. Had he forgotten to sign his name when he was there with me that night and just went back to sign it later? That didn't seem like too far of a stretch, I guess. I myself had forgotten to sign the sheet this morning.

I hated questioning Miles' intentions so I settled on that explanation for now, knowing I could easily ask him later. I was overreacting because of the whole Frances thing. But as Headmistress Craw's voice droned on around me a question did creep into my mind that I hadn't thought of before. The panic of seeing Lillian in the hospital bed distracted me at the time. The nurses weren't the ones to alert me that Lillian was in the medical ward. Miles was. How did he know Lillian was hurt in the first place? The nurses wouldn't have called him. A wave of frigid air whooshed through me. This situation was an all-too-familiar ghost of the night Laura was murdered. Miles was the first to know that night, too.

Class passed quickly while I was wrapped up in my own thoughts. Once everyone was dismissed, the class dwindled down and soon Frances and I were the only ones left in the room. I glanced down at my pen and completely blank piece of paper and shoved both into my textbook.

"Have a wonderful day, Headmistress Craw," Frances cooed as she gathered up her books and turned to walk out. She did not glance in my direction as she left. I remained seated. Headmistress Craw didn't acknowledge my presence. In fact, she didn't look up for the notes she was writing for a full five minutes. I watched the minutes on the clock behind her desk tick by silently. When Craw finally did look up, she locked eyes with me for only a moment before walking across the room to grab a book and bring it back to her desk. After a few more minutes of silence passed, I started to wonder if she still wanted me to stay. My face burned as I realized I was already late for my meeting with Professor Howard. It was apparent she did not plan to acknowledge that I was still sitting here. So, I slid my book back in my bag and stood.

"Ms. Parker, did I say you were dismissed?" her voice echoed in the empty room even though she wasn't yelling.

"Uh...no...I just-" I slowly moved towards her desk. She still hadn't looked up from her book.

"You just what? You thought it appropriate to have a confrontation with a fellow student *during* my class?" she demanded, her voice like ice, her milky eyes burning a hole through me. A chill ran down my spine. I couldn't put my finger on exactly what about Craw made a streak of terror run through me nearly every time I saw her eyes. It was probably because of the tales she told in class, the fact that she had witnessed every one of the horror stories she told. The fact that she was an open worshiper of the Fallen Angel. I tried very hard not to have a prejudice against her since a large portion of the witch community openly worshiped the Fallen Angel. Even Professor Howard worshipped him. But there was something about hearing the terrors Craw had witnessed. I could never quite push them out of my mind when I saw her. She lifted her eyebrow, awaiting my response.

"No. It was not appropriate, ma'am," I admitted.

"And why did you think you could dismiss yourself after

I specifically asked you to stay, hmm?" she questioned, peering at me over her glasses. I regretted ever wondering if she was going to acknowledge my presence and wished she would go back to focusing on her book. Silence was much better than this.

"I-I," I stuttered. I paused to take a breath and collect my thoughts before continuing. Letting her see me sweat was embarrassing. "I thought you may not want to talk to me. I wasn't sure. And I'm late for my weekly consultation so I..."

As if on cue, the door to the classroom creaked open to reveal Professor Howard standing on the other side. "Ah, there she is!" he cheered. "I was beginning to worry." He made his way down the aisle to stand beside me, facing Craw.

"Greetings, Professor Howard. Is this your pupil?" she questioned with an eyebrow raised and her lips pursed.

"Yes, she is. I have been waiting for her to show up for our weekly consultation," he responded, smiling in my direction undoubtedly trying to ease the tension in the air.

"Ah. Well, I needed to speak with Ms. Parker for a moment. She thought it necessary to confront another student in my classroom. Very inappropriate, wouldn't you agree?" She was no longer looking at Professor Howard. She was glaring at me.

"Really?" Howard asked with a genuinely confused look on his face. He crossed his arms, wrinkling his tight, cream jacket. "That does not seem like Josie. May I ask who the student was?"

"Frances Barns," Craw said, tilting her head. "I understand she is also another one of your pupils." Now it was Professor Howard who was in the line of fire. Two students he meets with on a weekly basis exchanging heated words in the Headmistress' class was not a good look for him. Suddenly, I felt guilty for my outburst. I was not sorry I had confronted Frances but acting on impulse proved to be nearly ineffective anyway. All it did was fluster Frances and strengthen my theory. I still didn't have any concrete evidence. I should have thought further ahead. Usually I would have talked to Lillian before I did something as big as calling out Frances in a room full of people, but Lillian was in a hospital bed. And now my thoughtlessness was harming Professor Howard.

To my surprise, Howard looked unfazed. "Yes, she is. I am meeting with her later in the day. Perhaps I'll be able to get to the bottom of this if you would be so kind as to excuse the two of us." He nodded in my direction.

"As you are well aware, I tolerate no nonsense inside and outside of the classroom, Professor Howard. I also do not tolerate secrets, as you and Professor Rose are well aware." My heart all but stopped. What was Craw implying? "When, not if, you 'get to the bottom of this,'" Craw raised her hands to do air quotes, "I expect you will come see me. Since these two young ladies both meet with you, I trust you to sort out this mess."

Professor Howard shoved his hands in his pockets and nodded, keeping his lips pressed in a hard line. She turned her attention back to me. "Ms. Parker, you are not off the hook. I will speak with you later."

"Yes, Headmistress Craw. Again, I apologize for my behavior," I said in a very small voice.

"Do not let it happen again." Her delicate voice turned demanding. She broke eye contact to look at her book again. She began flipping the pages, so Professor Howard and I took that as our dismissal. We both scurried down the aisle and out the door without another word.

Hallow's Eve was in full effect as we entered the garden. I was not feeling very festive at the minute, but the decorations covering every inch of the garden were hard to ignore. Orange and black lights twinkled in rows hanging above our heads. Jack-o'-lanterns with the school's logo carved in the front were lit up and sitting on every bench. It was a gloomy day, the sky filled with dark, looming clouds, so you could see the light from them illuminating the garden despite it being midday. I wasn't sure if the grim weather was natural or if a spell had been placed on the clouds surrounding the island. A sunny day wasn't suitable for Hallow's Eve. We passed by Laura's memorial, the flowers still in full bloom and I sighed.

Professor Howard and I walked side-by-side in silence. I wondered if he was embarrassed by the mention of his relationship with Professor Rose or if he was just contemplating what to say to me. Maybe he was angry I got him scolded.

When we reached his office, I felt relieved. Despite the figures of the Fallen Angel, which usually made me uncomfortable, I felt at ease. This room felt like a safe haven at the moment. I sat down in my usual chair and waited for Professor Howard to speak. He didn't for a while. He merely sat in silence at his desk, adjusting one of his figures, even though it appeared to already be in the proper place. I could hear the minutes ticking by on his clock adorning the wall and tried to focus on that sound instead of allowing my thoughts to go wild again.

"So," he cleared his throat, "what is going on with you and Ms. Barnes?"

"It's a little complicated," I stalled, feeling exposed all of the sudden. I acted irrationally and now I would have to explain my thinking to a Professor I respected. The fact that I flipped out because of a name on a paper seemed very silly now. Surely, he would think I was insane.

"I'm sure I can keep up, Josie," he said gravely. Howard obviously wasn't going to let this go. "Honestly, this does not seem like you at all. I am concerned."

"I feel overwhelmed, I guess. I don't know if you heard, but Lillian was attacked and she's still in a coma as far as I know." I looked down at my hands as I spoke, hoping he wouldn't think I was using Lillian's situation as an excuse. It was actually true that her attack led to this whole mess. I felt like I needed to defend my best friend. And if she were awake, she would have stopped me before it got too far.

"Ah, yes. I did hear," he said as if he suddenly understood everything. "I'm sure that is difficult. Especially considering it is almost the anniversary of your mother's death." His blunt statement sent a shock through my spine and my eyes shot up from my hands. He *was* right. My mother died three days after Hallow's Eve. But I pushed that out of my mind every year by keeping myself distracted with anything I could find. Lillian usually helped with that.

Professor Howard had never come right out and talked about her actual death this way. He always waited for me to bring it up. I felt unjustified anger. What gave him the right to bring up my mother?

"Like it or not, you come from a bloodline that has some of the most powerful witches of all time," he continued. "You may not understand this now, but because of that, you always have eyes on you. You need to hold yourself to a higher standard." I hated him saying this. Not that he wasn't right about my family, but his cold tone made me feel as if he were saying that my mother wouldn't be proud of my behavior. And that was none of his business.

"You cannot have an outburst in class," he said sternly. "Craw will see that as a sign of weakness. She needs to know you are capable of controlling your emotions. If you cannot be trusted to control your own emotions, how can you be trusted to control your remarkable powers?" He nearly rolled his eyes. "You are meant for great things, Josie. Do not throw them away over some disagreement with a classmate."

He took a deep breath and I felt like the lecture was over. I tried to take in what he said objectively instead of stewing in anger. I guess he had a point. Was I capable of controlling my powers if they were as powerful as he said? I didn't feel any different than my other classmates, but no adult seemed to think I was average. Miles even said students knew about my family. If they were right and I really was as gifted as people say, then Howard was right, too. I needed to practice control.

"What was the disagreement about, anyway?" he asked, his tone softer now.

"It seems silly now." I took a deep breath and caved. "I saw Frances' name on the sign-in sheet at the hospital ward. I wanted to know who she was there to see even though I suppose it wasn't my business. So, I confronted her. I knew she had to be there for Lillian, and I couldn't understand why. I reacted without thinking in Craw's class." I shook my head, trying to clear the memory of me yelling at Frances out.

Professor Howard immediately transformed his face to stone, attempting to hide any emotions he was feeling, but I could see a glint of rage hiding behind his eyes. My shoulder tensed. He was angry with me. He thought I was irrational and probably immature. I hated disappointing people.

"I see," he said with clenched teeth. "Well, have you sorted it out with Ms. Barnes?" His voice was controlled.

"I guess so." I paused. "I know it was foolish to react that way and I'm sorry Craw came after you for my mistake." He nodded and his face relaxed a bit. Perhaps an apology was all he needed.

"Well, we are running late so we will finish this conversation next week." He stood abruptly, so I made my way to the door and Professor Howard followed. When I opened it, Frances was biting her nails and pacing in the hallway in front of the entrance to Howard's office. She stopped in her tracks when she saw us. I expected her to make a snide comment since I had gotten in trouble or, at the very least, smirk, but instead she looked nervous.

Her eyes glazed past me and went straight to Professor Howard. I glanced in his direction before turning to leave. He was glaring at Frances. If looks could kill, she would be long gone. He must be angry with her, too. That didn't make much sense to me, though. Craw didn't seem mad at Frances. Why should Howard be? Unless Professor Howard saw through her innocent act just like I did. I tried not to smile when I thought of Howard lecturing her like he had just done to me.

"I'm sorry for my behavior today, Frances," I mumbled as I walked past her. I didn't really mean it, but I wanted to put all of this behind me. Frances still didn't acknowledge my presence. She walked straight into the office with her head hung low. The door practically slammed behind her. I stood in the hallway alone. There were no other students around. No noise. Just me and the silence. In that moment, I knew I had never been more alone.

11

A NIGHT TO REMEMBER

I collapsed on my bed feeling exhausted. My body wasn't tired, but my mind was. My head had not stopped spinning since I saw that sign-in sheet this morning. I still had so many questions, but no one to talk to. My heart throbbed. I *needed* Lillian here. I couldn't make it through without her. She was the only person I trusted without a shadow of a doubt. And probably the only person who wouldn't think I was absolutely bonkers for being so concerned about Frances visiting the medical wing.

My head started spinning with all my thoughts. Frances had no reason to suddenly develop some friendship with Lillian while she was in a coma. She hated Lillian nearly as much as she hated me. Why was Professor Howard so angry at Frances after our meeting? He basically slammed the door after she stepped inside his office. Why was Miles' name *after* mine on the sign-in sheet? Had he simply forgotten to write it down when he arrived? That seemed reasonable to me, but was I just seeing what I *wanted* to see? My brain was so foggy I wasn't sure I could trust my own judgment.

At least I knew I could ask Miles about it at the dance tonight. I glanced over at my dress hanging on the outside of my closet. Lillian's dress was hanging on hers, but she wouldn't be wearing it. This was too much to process for one day, so I rolled over on my side and closed my eyes. Maybe a nap would clear the fuzz in my head. I fell asleep on a pillow wet with tears.

* * *

I heard a door slam and opened my eyes slowly. My head was still fuzzy, despite the nap, and now my arm was tingling. I pulled it out from under my pillow and it flopped down on my bed limply. I moved it around to try and wake it up but wasn't having much luck. A nap had not helped at all.

"Oops. Were you asleep?" Ava asked even though she already knew the answer. My hair was disheveled, and I was pretty sure I had lines on the right side of my face from sleeping on my arm. I didn't answer. I just groaned, looked at the clock, and flopped back down on my blankets. My roommates had obviously come back to get ready for the dance. Miles would be at my door, dressed to the nines, to pick me up in a mere two hours.

I could have spent the full two hours making sure I looked perfect, but I was much too comfy and one hour would be plenty of time to get ready. So, I pulled the covers over my head. I wasn't ready to stare at Lillian's dress hanging on her closet, ready to be worn. It wouldn't be taken off the hanger tonight and it didn't feel right going to this dance without her. She had been my date for this dance every year since we'd been at North End. This year would have been different regardless since I had a real date, but I wouldn't have let Lillian feel left out. I would have made sure she made every picture with us. We would have all three danced together on the floor. Lillian would have made sure I had plenty of distractions from the upcoming anniversary I dreaded so much, just like she always did. It would have been fun.

I listened to my roommates gossiping about who was going with who tonight, wondering if anyone would ask them to dance, and comparing their list of girls who had uglier dresses than them. I loved my roommates. They were kind to me and very easy to live with, but their conversations were enough to drive me up the wall sometimes, especially today. We didn't share the same outlook on life. Their roommate was in the medical ward and *this* was all they could talk about. If

Lillian could overhear this conversation, she would be rolling her eyes just like me.

When I couldn't stand to hear their blabbering any longer, I crawled out from under my covers, grabbed my bathroom supplies, and trudged down the hall. The bathroom was packed, of course. Girls were running around with dresses in their hands, makeup smeared all over their faces, and rollers pinned in their hair. I squeezed through the crowd to one open mirror on the very end of the row. I splashed water on my face. It was freezing and helped clear my foggy mind a bit. I started putting on my makeup, more than I ever wore on an average day, and listened to the girls beside me.

The one standing up was already in her dress. It was skintight and neon green. And short to boot. I was sure if she turned around, I would nearly be able to see her butt cheeks. She looked good, but I couldn't imagine the dress would be very comfortable to dance in. Her makeup was already caked on and her hair was in rollers. She was dousing her friend's head in hairspray and teasing it with a comb. I wasn't sure what year they were, but I knew they couldn't be final years. Final years never tried this hard.

"Gracie, you are going to look uhhhh-mazing! Kelly won't be able to keep her hands off you!" the girl in the green dress exclaimed.

"You think? We might even leave the dance early." She

winked at her friend in the mirror.

"You are so bad!" green dress exclaimed. They both giggled.

"What about you, Sammi? Miles will *die* when he sees you! He'll leave that girl so quick she won't know what hit her! I don't care how powerful--Hey!" She jerked forward like her friend had elbowed her in the back. Miles. They were talking about *my* Miles. And her friend must have recognized me. Who were these girls? Interested in *my* boyfriend. The girl in the seat must have realized her mistake because I heard her mumble "oops" under her breath.

I felt the anger building up inside my chest, rising like bile in my throat. I felt the same way I had when I confronted Frances this morning. I opened my mouth to ask the girls why they were talking about my boyfriend but stopped before anything came out. I remembered what Professor Howard said. I needed to keep my emotions in check. I could not lash out on others because I was going through something terrible. Normally, a small comment from some random girl in a bathroom wouldn't cause me to bat an eye, but I was seriously on edge. I counted to 10 in my head and took three deep breaths.

There is no reason to be angry, I told myself. *Miles would not be interested in this girl even if I wasn't in the picture.* It was true. It had nothing to do with her short skirt or makeup. Honestly, in weak moments of insecurity, I wished I had the confidence someone like her had. She could rock an outfit I would never even look at in a store. But Miles was deeper than the surface and I doubt he would be interested in a girl who would attempt to steal another girl's boyfriend. That wasn't kind. And that was Miles' favorite thing about me.

I bit my lip and hung my head. My behavior today had *not* been kind. I was immediately glad I held my tongue instead of confronting the girls next to me. All this was making me crazy. I couldn't wait to see Miles so I would feel more like myself. I rushed through the rest of my makeup and curled the ends of my hair. I asked the girls beside me if I could borrow their hairspray and they let me without a second thought, and I realized I may have judged them too harshly. I tipped my hair over and sprayed my whole head. When I looked in the mirror, my hair was lush and curly. My green eyes sparkled, and flecks of gold shone through. My gold eyeshadow brought out the new color. The makeup hid the dark circles under my eyes and my lips were painted a deep red. I borrowed the color from Lillian's makeup bag. I looked like a normal person. At least I didn't appear as manic as I felt.

When I got back to the room, Ava and Daliah were already dressed and ready to go. "Josie, we're going to go to a pregame party on the third floor if you want to join," Daliah offered. She always made sure to invite me anytime they had plans, even if I didn't accept the offer every time. I appreciated that.

"Thank you for inviting me, Daliah, but Miles is supposed to be here soon. Have fun!" They hurried out the door. Even if Miles wasn't coming, I wouldn't have joined them on this particular outing. Dances were the exception to the usually moderate alcohol consumption on campus. People tended to get a little wild this time of year. The pregame parties consisted of mass amounts of alcohol and that wasn't really my thing on any day, but especially not tonight. With my mindset, if I had anything to drink tonight, I would probably end up scratching an innocent person's eyes out because they poured me the wrong drink.

I was glad to have the room to myself while I got ready. I looked at Lillian's impossibly small dress hanging on her closet. It was fiery red, almost the exact shade of her hair. It was short and petite like her, with a glittery top and feathers decorating the bottom. It would have fallen just past her knees. It was the perfect dress, and she had known so as soon as she tried it on. I turned my attention to my dress and felt overwhelmed by my gratitude for Professor Rose once again. It was more beautiful than any dress I had ever owned.

As I ran my fingers over the material, I saw something float to the floor. A piece of paper. I bent down to pick up what I assumed would be a receipt but was surprised when I saw a signature. "Rose." I picked up the slightly wrinkled paper and read it out loud. It was a note.

Josie,

You are a very special young lady, just like your mother. She would want you to have this. Have a lovely evening.

Rose

I held the note to my chest for a moment, feeling tears stinging my eyes, before walking to my nightstand and sliding the note in a small, green box in the drawer. There were few items in this box. I reserved it for special things, like my mother's engagement ring, a card my father bought me on my 13th birthday, and a note Miles wrote me after our first date. This note seemed more than worthy enough to be included in my collection.

I walked back to my closet and slipped my dress over my head carefully, trying not to smudge my makeup, and turned to look in the only mirror we had in our room. I ran my hands along the lace on the top half, taking in each small detail of the dress. It was long sleeved, and the lace ran until it hit my hips. Then it was only black silk flowing all the way to the ground. I stared at myself for a while thinking of how strange it was that the person in the mirror was me. My outer appearance was so different from the 13-year-old girl who lost her mother those years ago. Mom would hardly recognize me now. My heart yearned for her to be standing beside me, but I knew if there was any way she could see me now she would be watching. Surely the Divinity would allow her to peek through the veil to the mortal world on a night like tonight. I closed my eyes and imagined she was here, picturing her soft features. Her pale skin would be flushed from a wide smile. Her pastel green eyes would sparkle with tears, but not from sadness. From joy. Her light brown hair would be pulled into its usual low bun, and she and Dad would laugh as they snapped pictures of me in ridiculous poses around the room. I heard a knock at the door and my eyes popped open, tearing me away from my perfect dream. I slipped on my heels before rushing to answer it.

I opened the door to a huge bouquet of black roses—the official flower of Hallow's Eve. Miles popped his head out from behind them. He wore a huge smile as he said, "Happy Hallow's Eve!" in a deep, spooky voice. His smile faded as he looked me up and down. "Whoa," he whispered and shook his head quickly as if he was shaking himself out of some sort of trance. "Uh-wow. You look incredible."

"Thank you," I smiled feeling the blood rush to my cheeks. "So do you." I looked him up and down and only felt wonderment. What in the world was this beautiful boy doing with me? His hair was pinned back again, and I had almost decided it was my favorite way he wore his hair. His suit was completely black, even down to his undershirt. His eyes were blue again.

He handed me the flowers, and I said, "Thank you, again." I was never a sucker for flowers before. My dad never got them for my mom. She said they were pointless since they would only wilt and die. I always felt the same way until the first time Miles brought me the flowers that still sat by my bed. They hadn't wilted or died thanks to his charm, but even if they had it wouldn't have mattered to me. The thought of him going out of his way to make me feel special was enough to change my opinion on flowers forever.

"Are you ready?" He held out his arm and I wrapped mine around it.

"Ready." As we walked through the halls of the castle, we passed several other couples. Some were wrapped up in each other, obviously part of a long-term relationship, others were barely holding hands, perhaps a first date, and a few were clearly just two friends who decided to go together. I wondered what people thought of me and Miles. Did they think we were serious or just a flame that would fizzle out?

As we walked, he asked me about my day and Lillian. I wasn't fully ready to question him on why his name was signed below mine on the sign-in sheet. I felt pure bliss in this moment and bringing up risky topics would only spoil my mood. I could not bear that thought since this was the happiest I had felt since the night Lillian went missing. I wanted to enjoy this without my paranoia getting in the way. So, I avoided that conversation. Instead, I decided to tell him about the incident in the bathroom.

"I have something funny to tell you," I whispered. The girls from the bathroom were in line to enter the ballroom a few groups ahead of us. I could see the girl who was interested in Miles peeking at us in a not-so-discreet manner. Miles looked down at me and raised his eyebrows, curious. "I was getting ready in the bathroom and a girl was talking about her hopes to steal you away from me tonight."

"Oh, really?" he laughed, appearing to be genuinely shocked. "Doesn't she know that would be an impossible task?"

"'Impossible' is a strong word," I said without thinking, allowing my insecurities to sneak through. I could have kicked myself after. That was the exact opposite thing to say if you really trust someone.

"I don't think so," he said, unfazed. "I'm all yours, Josie." He leaned down and kissed my cheek. My skin tingled as he pulled away. I racked my brain for something romantic to say back. I wasn't as good with words as Miles, so I simply said, "I feel the same" and hoped it expressed the deep feelings for him that swallowed every part of me.

When we made it to the front of the line, we stopped under the archway to take a picture, like all the other couples were doing. There were twinkling yellow lights hanging behind us and orange and black balloons covering the floor. We did a few poses, ending with one where Miles attempted to lift me over his head. He didn't even come close, but we were howling with laughter by the time we got our snapshots.

The gym was decorated in its classic way. Tons of lights, balloons, jack-o'-lanterns and ghosts—a nod to the human world. Sculptures of the Divinity and Fallen Angel also decorated the room to represent our world. In previous years, I felt almost invisible when I walked into this ballroom, which didn't bother me too much since I was instantly anxious anytime I was the center of attention. Only one boy had ever asked me to dance at these events and no heads previously turned when I entered the room, but this year was different. As I glided into the ballroom on Miles' arm, I couldn't help but notice several heads turning to gaze in our direction. It made me feel slightly uncomfortable as I would have expected, but strangely proud at the same time because I had a feeling that the heads were not turning for me. Rather, it was my date who was the object of everyone's affection. And I was the object of his.

In the middle of the room, the disco ball spun as couples

wrapped their arms around each other for the first slow song of the night. "Make You Feel My Love" by Bob Dylan played on the speakers. Miles held out his hand and I took it. He led me to the middle of the dance floor. I draped my arms around his shoulders and my heels were so high that our lips were closer than they had ever been. His hands found their way to my waist. We swayed side to side without saying a word, just looking into each other's eyes. Miles took one hand from my hip and placed it on my cheek. If my heart beat much faster, surely it would explode. It was hard to describe how I felt. The wholeness swelled in my chest making it difficult to inhale and I imagined this is what people meant when they said something took their breath away.

I was sure Miles felt it, too, whatever this feeling was. "I'm so in love with you," he murmured, leaning his lips down, just a little, to press them into mine. He pulled his lips away, but his face stayed close to mine. I pressed my forehead against his and closed my eyes, basking in this feeling.

"I'm in love with you, too, Miles," I sighed. The song ended too soon, but the feeling in my chest remained. A fast-paced song came on next. Several students cheered and backed away from their dates to start dancing, but I couldn't pull myself away from Miles. Even as the dance floor flooded with more students coming from the sidelines I couldn't look away. A boy who had obviously been to a pregame party was dancing so wildly he bumped into us, nearly toppling over. He steadied himself and kept going without even noticing us. Miles and I laughed and were finally able to pull away from each other. I took a deep breath and let it out loudly.

"Punch?" I asked, pointing to the table set up to the side. It was overflowing with snacks and drinks.

"Yeah," Miles agreed. We drank two cups each and spent the next 30 minutes laughing and dancing like fools. There was no way we looked good, but it was fun. Maybe the most fun I'd had all school year. We both worked up a sweat so while Miles ran to the restroom, I grabbed another glass of punch. I sipped on my Hallow's Eve themed cup slowly, taking the time to notice the orange background with bat outlines splattered across it, until I saw Frances crossing the room. My heart leapt to my throat. She looked like a model in her four-inch heels. Her dress was short and silver with slinky straps. She looked very similar to the disco ball hanging from the ceilings, but she still walked towards me with confidence. *Oh, crap*, I thought. Here we go.

"Josie," Frances said, stopping in front of me. She was impossibly tall in her heels. Even taller than Miles. I had to tilt my head up to look her in the eyes. I sat my cup down on the table and crossed my arms, preparing myself for whatever was coming next. "I just wanted to say...I'm sorry. About everything."

My mouth nearly dropped open as the words left her lips. I searched her face for any hint of sarcasm, but I could see none. She seemed genuine. This could not be real.

"I know I haven't been the nicest person these past couple of years," Frances continued, not taking her eyes off mine. "Honestly, I always felt a little...jealous," she nearly choked on the word, "of you and your family. Your history is...well, you have some of the most powerful witches of all time in your bloodline. I made it into a competition when it never needed to be one." I waited patiently for the punchline with my arms still crossed. "And when Lillian was attacked, I felt terrible for the way I treated her, too. I was scared I would never have a chance to apologize. So, your suspicions were right today. I went to see her. I knew then and there that I needed to apologize for my behavior. So, this is me apologizing and hoping we can put all of this behind us." This had to be tormenting for her to say, but she got through it without a single sarcastic word. Maybe she actually meant it...

I was silent for a beat. Did I really *want* to forgive Frances and be her friend? No. But it took guts for her to say this to me. The least I could do is forgive and forget...mostly.

"Yeah, of course," I said. "We witches need to stick together, now more than ever. All is forgiven." It truly wouldn't be such a bad thing to have Frances on my team. Even though she wasn't the most likeable *person*, she was an extremely talented witch.

"Thank you for your kindness." She smiled an actual smile and walked away. I felt shocked as I watched her go and wondered what class would be like now that she didn't hate me. No more snide remarks, no more dirty looks from across the room, no more spells that made me nearly miss class. It was a relief honestly.

I felt someone hug me from behind and smelled Miles' cologne instantly. As I turned around to kiss him, I heard my favorite song blast over the speakers. I pulled away and gasped. "Let's go!" I grabbed my drink and chugged the rest before taking off.

When we got to the middle of the dance floor, we were swallowed by a sea of other students heading to boogie. We were packed in like sardines, but I managed to throw my hands above my head and sing along, even though the music was so loud not even I could hear my voice. I danced harder than I had all night. Unfortunately, halfway through the song, I started feeling light-headed. It was very stuffy in the middle of the crowd of people dancing and I was feeling claustrophobic. The air was too muggy to breathe properly. "Can we go sit down for a second?" I yelled over the booming music.

"Sure. Are you feeling okay? You don't look so good," Miles said in a concerned tone. He put his arm around my waist as we pushed through the crowd and off the dance floor.

"I'm okay," I assured him as he guided me to an empty seat. He sat down beside me. "I just danced too hard, I guess," I laughed weakly. I felt better now that I was sitting. I wiped my forehead and realized I was sweating.

"Do you need anything? I can get you water," Miles offered, but I didn't want him to leave my side. The fuzziness was returning, and I didn't want to be alone.

"No, no. Please, don't leave." I licked my lips trying to get rid of the dry feeling in my mouth without water. Why was I so thirsty all of the sudden? I had three cups of punch tonight. *Maybe someone spiked the punch with alcohol,* I giggled to myself and Miles raised one eyebrow. Suddenly, the sign-in sheet popped into my head and for some reason I wasn't too worried to ask about it. So, I blurted out, "Did you go see Lillian after me the other day?"

"Huh?" He looked confused.

"The other day..." Were my words slurring together? "Your name was on the sign out sheet after mine, but I left *after* you. It was right above Frances'. And you knew she was in the medical ward before me. Suspicious."

"Josie, look at me." He put his hand under my chin to tilt it up. "I overheard a guard mentioning her name on my way to class that morning. When I knew for sure it was her, I messaged you. And yes, I went to see Lillian again. I had gone to the church of the Divinity after I left you to pray for her to wake up and I had a good feeling after. I just wanted to see if it worked." My head drooped again, and he lifted it back up gently. "Seriously, Josie, you don't look good." I couldn't think straight enough to even guess what was wrong with me.

"I don't feel so great. Can you walk me to the bathroom?" I asked, slowly. Maybe if I splashed some water on my face it would snap me out of this. I didn't want the night to end, but if I didn't start feeling better, I needed to leave. And probably head straight to the medical wing.

Miles walked me to the exit and guided me down the hall, keeping his arm around me the whole time. My eyes felt heavy. "Did you eat anything today?" he asked as we walked.

I tried to remember if I had lunch or not, but it seemed impossible to remember anything at all. "I don't think I've been eating much since Lillian..." I trailed off as we approached the bathroom door.

"I will be right outside this door, then we're leaving. Call my name if you need help," Miles said as he slowly released me. I nodded and walked into the bathroom. It was hard to walk on my own, and I was out of breath right away. My vision was blurry, and I felt so dizzy. I leaned on the wall for support and caught my breath before stumbling to the sink. I clamped my hands down on the edges. Hard. My head was spinning.

"What is wrong with me?" I asked myself out loud in the mirror. Then it hit me like a ton of bricks. My chest tightened.

The punch. Frances came to talk to me while I was drinking the punch. "Apologize," I scoffed to myself. I had sat my drink on the table while she was "apologizing." What if she put something in it?

As I gazed at my reflection, it looked like I had three heads swaying back and forth. "This is weird," I laughed to myself. I started the faucet and attempted to splash water on my face, but I missed, and it spilled it on my dress. I giggled to myself again. *Wait, this is not funny. Professor Rose bought this for me.* My thoughts were all over the place. *Miles*, I thought. *I need Miles.* I needed to tell him about Frances. I pictured him standing outside the bathroom door waiting for me. I used the image of his perfect face as motivation to force my feet to move. *It's working. It's working. It's…* Everything went black.

12
THE BLACK FOREST

I blinked several times trying to clear my vision. Something wet was in one of my eyes, matting my lashes together. Did I drool in my sleep? My head was throbbing, and I had a bad taste in my mouth. *Yuck!* This was the worst nap ever. My head was still fuzzy like I was trapped in a dream. *I need to wake up,* I told myself, still unable to see. I let my eyes close again, and I began to drift back into the dream. It was too hard to wake. Sleep felt better. *No,* I grumbled to myself again. *Miles will be here any minute.* My heart stopped beating for a moment. *Miles?* I already saw him. At the dance. Wait, did I already go to the dance?

A flood of memories came rushing back: Our silly picture before we entered the ballroom. The way Miles whispered my name during our slow dance. The punch. *The punch!* I gasped loudly, forcing my eyes to peel open. The liquid dripped in my left eye and it stung. I refused to close them, though. I wasn't safe in my bed. I wasn't on the bathroom floor where everything went black.

I assessed my situation, frantically, realizing the danger. I was sitting upright in a chair. There were cables wrapped around my arms as if to pin me down, but even if they weren't there, I wouldn't have been able to move anything below my shoulders. Some sort of a spell had obviously been cast, leaving me momentarily paralyzed. My mind flashed back to Headmistress Craw's class. She had seen the paralysis spell with her own eyes and taught it to us. I had practiced the words. I felt sick to my stomach. Glancing down, I saw I was still wearing my dress from the dance but was missing a heel. There was a vibrant red splattered on one of my lace sleeves. I turned my head in a less than comfortable way to see where the color came from. *Blood*. Was I bleeding?

I wasn't alone. Sitting straight across from me was Headmistress Craw. I felt furious when I saw her. She was the one that taught this spell to students at the school, and I had a horrible feeling it was a student who was behind all of this. A student who was in my class. A student who used a fake apology to take advantage of me.

Headmistress Craw was slumped down in her chair, unconscious, but she had cables wrapped around her just like

I did. Since she was slumped down, I could see the side of her head, the way it was gashed open. She had been hit with something. And very recently. The wound was too large to heal itself. Blood was dripping on the ground slowly. *Drip. Drip. Drip.*

"Headmistress," I hissed as quietly as I could manage. Despite the anger I felt towards her at the moment, I knew she was my only chance to make it out of this. "Headmistress Craw, please." I heard the hysteria slipping into my voice. It shook. I tried in vain to kick my feet.

I stared at the pool of blood forming on the ground. It covered the leaves that were scattered on the dirt. I looked around, beyond my immediate surroundings, for the first time. I knew where I was. The Black Forest. Exactly *where* in the Black Forest was a mystery, but I recognized the tall trees. I turned my head as far around as possible looking for some sight of the castle, but there was nothing. Nothing but monstrous trees all around me. There was a glint of light to my left, but the dripping blood made it hard to see. I also felt heat coming from that direction. There was a fire. But who set it ablaze?

Someone was out here with us. Frances was already in my mind. She must be behind this. I already knew she spiked my punch. She was messing with me. She meant what she said when she admitted her jealousy of me and my family and was punishing me for being gifted. Payback for having a powerful family. What kind of sick revenge was this? And if it was revenge, why did she bring Headmistress Craw out here, too?

A sick feeling sunk in as I heard voices approaching. My heart started to race, and my breath came in small, short spurts. I was panicking. I tried to move my arms, but it was useless. *Oh no! Oh no!* If I could not remain calm, I could die here. I forced myself to breathe slowly so I could listen to the voices approaching. They weren't whispering which meant one thing: we were nowhere near the castle. They weren't worried about being heard. I recognized one voice immediately. I wasn't surprised when I heard Frances' deep voice cooing to whoever the other person was. It was a man's voice, that much I could tell. I even recognized the voice. I had heard it somewhere before, but I couldn't hear well enough to place it. Who was evil enough to participate in...whatever this was?

Their feet dragged along, crunching on leaves. Their voices stopped, but I got the sense they were close to me. The pair paused in front of the fire and I saw their shadows: Frances' tall, slender body with her long limbs reaching out to touch the unidentified man's face. She caressed it lovingly. "I'm sorry. I love you," I heard her murmur.

"I love you, too, my devil," said Professor Howard, with a hint of annoyance in his voice. My heart sank to my feet. I could have thrown up. *Professor Howard?*

The two love birds moved from the fire to step directly in front of me. It was true. Professor Howard was standing in the middle of the Black Forest with his arm wrapped around Frances' waist. The betrayal cut deep, and if I wasn't wrapped to the chair, I probably would have collapsed. I trusted this man. I spoke with him *every* single week about school, my friends, my *parents*. I would have never guessed he was capable of this. Professor Howard stared down at me smirking, and his eyes looked like I had never seen them. They were dark. Maybe it was because we were out in the woods at night or maybe it was because they were dead. I saw no emotion except anger and no color except black.

I imagined his smirk came from my shock. He was pleased. I didn't want him to know what I was feeling, but my face had, no doubt, already betrayed me. *No.* I would not give him the satisfaction. I turned my face to stone, forcing the numbness I felt in my limbs to spread to my cheeks and lips and eyes, so it was only my heart, concealed and secret, that ached. His smirk disappeared. Irritation replaced it.

"Hi, Josie," Frances smiled and waved at me as casually as if we were passing each other in the halls. "I'm so glad we're friends now." My face remained stone even as the anger boiled my blood. I wanted to hit her, but my frozen body wouldn't allow it. "You never saw this coming, did you?"

"Frances, dear, can you stop talking to our sacrifices?" Professor Howard asked Frances while placing his hand gently on her cheek. I could hear a hint of exasperation in his voice, but he did his best to cover it with a sweet, calming tone, like pouring honey on a rash. One word from him was enough to make Frances close her mouth. She looked at the ground like she was a child that had just been scolded. Which I guess was pretty accurate.

The word "sacrifices" finally registered in my brain. I waited for the panic to come, but it did not. I kept my face stone, though my heart still felt betrayed. I suppose I could have guessed we were sacrifices. They busted the Headmistress' head and drugged me to get me here. It was obvious we weren't returning to North End after all this.

"I need to finish the calling spell. Can you take care of these two by yourself?" Howard asked as if he were speaking to an infant, obviously not confident in Frances' abilities.

"They are both under a paralysis spell and one is unconscious. I think I can handle it," she assured him, letting him know she was offended by his doubt. But I heard how her voice shook as she mumbled the last sentence. Frances wanted him to see her as a capable woman, but even she was still unsure. Professor Howard stepped out of my line of sight. I couldn't tell how far into the woods he walked, but it was far enough that the sound of his feet crunching leaves became too quiet for me to hear. Frances was pacing around our chairs, wringing her hands. She was nervous. I had to at least try to talk some sense into her.

"What are doing, Frances?" I asked, making my voice sound as innocent as possible.

"You two are sacrifices, didn't you hear?" She stopped pacing and whipped her head in my direction. Her voice was coated in sarcasm. She was still in her dress, and the fire glinted off it.

"Sacrifices for what? You're not the kindest person I know, but I never took you for a murderer." Which was true. I knew Frances had a mean streak and she wasn't above sabotage, but I never feared for my life in her company. I also never suspected Professor Howard would be capable of harm, though. Or that he was seeing Frances, not Professor Rose, secretly. My stomach churned at the thought of an older— much older—witch dating a student. There was a lot I had missed even when it was right in front of my face.

"I am not a *murderer*," she enunciated every word and started pacing again. "I am a *Follower*. I am devoted." The three words she was saying were synonymous. When she said "Follower," she meant she followed the Fallen Angel. And every Follower of the Fallen Angel had or would kill someone at some point in their lives. Followers thought this action was not only justified, but necessary.

If I wasn't paying attention, I wouldn't have noticed the way Frances couldn't stop pacing, the way her words shook, the way she wrung her hands uncontrollably.

"Why, though? *Why* do you have to sacrifice us?" I pleaded.

"It must be done. It is his will," Frances gazed at the full moon shining through the trees. She thought this is what the Fallen Angel wanted.

"Is that really all you know, Frances? Whose will is it really? The Fallen Angel's or Professor How--?" I whispered, still unsure of Howard's location. He could not overhear this conversation if I had any hope of surviving. It was clear who was in control.

She interrupted me frantically before I could finish. "Howard speaks to him. He has a direct line of communication. He has met with him several times. The Fallen Angel *wants* this," she justified.

"So, you're just going to follow blindly without any explanation of *why* you're killing someone? Without even seeing the Fallen Angel yourself?" I could see beads of sweat forming on her head. There were cracks in her logic. She felt guilty somewhere deep down.

"That is my...duty. That is f-faith," Frances stuttered. I could do this. I could change her mind. I just had to keep her talking.

"Did you kill that girl, Frances? Laura?"

"No," she answered quickly, whipping her head to look directly in my eyes. Her voice was low suddenly. "That was Howard. He needed power to perform this ceremony. So, he *had* to kill her. To make him stronger. Killing a witch makes you much stronger than before." I wasn't sure who she was trying to convince: me or herself.

"Frances, I think Howard may have lied to you. Killing a witch *does* give you more power, but only the amount of power that witch possesses. That girl did not have much power. She was only 13."

"You're a poor liar," she accused, looking at me with disgust.

"Do you know what else killing a young witch does?" I continued. She did not interrupt this time. She wanted to hear it. "It keeps you young. You steal their youth." Frances stopped pacing for a moment to process what I just said.

"Maybe so. Then that must be the Fallen Angel's will," she rationalized, starting to pace again. "You wouldn't understand. Not even I understand, but I follow. I obey. So one day I can meet the Fallen Angel myself. Howard assured me that if I helped him, he would make that happen."

I wasn't sure I wanted to know the answer to my next question, but with a lump in my throat, I asked anyway. "What about Lillian?" my voice was barely audible. "Was that you?" I tried to keep my face stone, but I could not stop a tear from falling down my cheek.

Frances' pace quickened. She rolled back her shoulders before looking me straight in the eyes and answering. "Yes. It was me."

The lump in my throat doubled in size and I could no longer keep my face stone. Frances attacked my best friend, tried to kill her. More tears poured down my face while my eyes burned through Frances. I saw red. "Is that why you went to see her, then? To finish the job?"

"No!" she yelled. Her voice echoed through the trees. I looked around quickly checking to see if Professor Howard had heard her. Frances was turning her head doing the same. When she felt sure he hadn't, she continued. "I went there because...I felt guilty, okay?" She put her hands on her hips and shook her head like she was ashamed. "Wilmot said I needed to kill to prove my loyalty, but I didn't want it to be her." I felt sick as I realized she was using Howard's first name. "I wanted to choose a first year student, one I didn't even know, but I was in the library with him that night. And Lillian heard us. So, Wilmot said it had to be her and it had to be right then. She could not escape or everything we worked for would be ruined. She would tell Craw. I couldn't even do it right," she scoffed at her own words with revulsion. "A part of me didn't want to kill her. It's not the same as killing a stranger or someone you barely know or someone you hate even. To kill someone you grew up with is barbaric." Her words were spilling out so quickly I could barely understand them. "But I had to do it. He said I must. So, I tried. And I panicked like an inexperienced child." She said the word "child" as if it made her sick. I had a feeling some of these words had not just come out of her mouth, but Professor Howard's, as well. "I told myself I went to see her in the hospital so I could finish the job, but that wasn't true. I felt guilty. I'm such a young fool!"

"You're not a fool!" I hissed. "How could anyone take another's life and not feel guilty?" Maybe if I reassured her, she would set me free. I could see the panic in her eyes, hear the doubt in her words, and she even admitted to feeling guilty herself. She was about to crack and if she did, she would let us go. But I had to do it before Professor Howard returned. If he came back, she would do whatever he said. He had some sort of a hold on her.

Frances stopped pacing and walked towards me. She stopped a few feet away from my chair. "I just want to make him happy," she said with tears in her eyes.

"The Fallen Angel or Professor Howard?" I asked.

She shrugged and shook her head like the answer was obvious. "Both."

In that moment, I had never felt sorrier for a person. Frances was being manipulated. She was too young to fully understand what was even happening to her. So was I. She thought Howard loved her, and she would do anything to please him. Even kill for the Fallen Angel.

"Have you ever seen the Fallen Angel, Frances?" I asked, even though I already knew the answer. A single tear slipped out of her eye and she took a ragged breath in. "Is there any way that Professor Howard could be...lying?" Frances gazed off into the forest like she was searching for him. She looked like a lost puppy. "Please," I whispered desperately. "You don't want to do this. Let us go." When she turned to face me again her tears had stopped. She started walking towards me, her hands already reaching for the ties that bound me to the chair. *Yes! Yes!* I thought. *She's going to undo the spell! She's going to—*

Before I could finish my secret celebration, a dark hooded figure appeared behind Frances. "Look out!" I screamed, but it was too late.

13
SALVATION

The hooded figure slugged Frances in the back of the head with a book. A book that had "M. Langley" etched on the cover. I watched her fall and it all seemed to go in slow motion. Her eyes rolled back when the book made contact with her head and her body seemed like it was detached from her mind. It crumpled on the way to the ground uncontrollably. She fell at my feet and a small pool of blood began forming beside my bare foot. As I wondered how a book could do that much damage, the hooded figure stepped forward with it clasped in his hands. The book cover was dark and wilted, just like the one I had seen in Miles' room the night of Laura's murder, but this book was much, much larger. Metal spikes decorated the cover. Some glinted in the moonlight, but others dripped blood. Fresh blood, belonging to Frances, painted the left side of the book, but there was more blood on the other side that had already dried. Clearly it did not belong to Frances.

The book doubled as a weapon and suddenly the liquid dripping in my eye made sense. We had all been knocked out by this book. By Professor Howard. A panic like I never knew was possible rose in my chest as he walked towards me. He shook the hood off of his head and scooped up Frances. I had no chance of escaping now. Frances had been scared. Weak. Unsure. Guilt-ridden. She didn't want to go through with this. She was under the control of Professor Howard. But I knew he would never be swayed. My imminent death became apparent, and I lost all control. I no longer cared if he saw my fear. My face could not hold stone. I couldn't even keep my thoughts straight.

He tied Frances to another chair in between me and Headmistress Craw and I started wailing. "Help! Someone please help us! Help!" Professor Howard said nothing. He didn't even look up from the knots he was tying into the rope wrapped around Frances. "He's going to kill us! Professor Howard is going to kill us!"

"Oh, shut *up*, Ms. Parker. No one can hear you." Frances was secured to the chair, so Professor Howard turned to face me. His voice was calm. "We are deep in the Black Forest, and even if we weren't, I'm not half-witted. I placed a silencer spell around us. We could be five feet from the castle, and no one would hear you." He chuckled although he seemed unamused.

"Lillian knows it's you. She knows what you're doing and she's alive. You won't be able to get away with it!" I yelled fervently. He laughed like he was *very* amused this time.

"Frances can't even keep her mouth shut when it's most important: telling our sacrifices the plan!" He rolled his eyes in her direction. "Never mind. Once I perform the ceremony it won't matter. If I need to, I will finish the job that Frances couldn't." He shot a disgusted look in her direction. "I will be King after tonight. I will do whatever I please."

King? "King" is what some Followers call the Fallen Angel. Howard was planning on reigning by the Fallen Angel's side? "And when I'm ruler of the Underworld, there will be none of this ridiculous free will for witches. The witching world will follow me or die, just as it should have always been." The last sentence was the first time he didn't sound calm. It cracked on the word "die," and his voice grew louder and louder with excitement or insanity. Probably both.

So, he wasn't planning on ruling *with* the Fallen Angel. He was planning to take his place. Only a maniac would think they could take down the Fallen Angel.

"You...can't...kill the Fallen Angel..." I said bewildered. I didn't know much about him other than what I discovered in the book from the library, but I knew this one thing for certain:

He was the most cunning witch there had ever been.

"Oh, you can do whatever you please if you have the right help. I will take over this world first, then become the new ruler and offer the Fallen Angel salvation." Professor Howard mumbled "opstupefacio," the paralysis spell we learned in class, as he directed his hands towards Frances' unconscious body. I felt guilty for blaming Headmistress Craw for teaching us this spell. It hadn't been a student paralyzing us at all.

I searched the trees all around me, trying to find whatever witches were helping him, but I saw no one. "Who would be crazy enough to help you do that?"

"You're a very curious girl, aren't you?" he asked. "I'll give you the shortened version since I'm about to take your life. I mean, what harm will it do?" He laughed maniacally and began pacing in circles around my chair with his head held high. He certainly had a big enough ego to think he could become one of the most powerful rulers there has ever been. "Many of the lost souls and demons in the Underworld are displeased with the Fallen Angel, but once you're in the Underworld, you cannot overturn your ruler. He has complete control over you. So, I broke down the barrier between our worlds and spoke with them in secret on several occasions. Gathered an army of sorts. I just summoned them to this very forest. They walk amongst us right now." He stepped forward and leaned down so his face was so close to mine that I could feel his warm breath when he spoke. "If we all channel our power together and use the right spell," he tapped the book that was still in his hands with one finger, "we can overthrow him." A grin spread across his face like he was a kid of Christmas.

"And these spirits are okay with *you* as their leader?" I twisted my face as far away from his as I could. "They're okay with no free will?" I asked, wondering if they even knew what kind of ruler they were electing.

"They don't have free will, Ms. Parker. Once you sign your soul over to the Fallen Angel in the Underworld, all hope for free will disappears." He shrugged and stood again, walking towards the fire. "They may not know all I plan to do," he mumbled more to himself than me. Of course, these souls had no idea what they were doing. They didn't understand the deception he was planning. Even Followers who sacrificed their soul to the devil didn't deserve what was coming their way. If I ever doubted the Fallen Angel's existence before, tonight that speculation disappeared. He *did* exist. But there were witches just as evil right here on Earth.

"Why did you lie to Frances? She didn't know any of this," I hissed.

Professor Howard calmly sighed. "I needed someone powerful, but not too powerful, to help me. Someone smart enough to know the school, but not smart enough to detect my lies. Someone desperate for love and approval. Someone who could be manipulated, who could be blamed if things went wrong. Frances was just the right girl." Howard winked at me and it made my skin crawl. "In the beginning, I did have hope she could be as wicked as some of the witches I've known. I thought we could rule together one day. But she is weak." He shook his head in disdain. "So, instead she will be part of the sacrifice that will make me ruler. I needed three abnormally powerful witches for this sacrifice. I need the power. And you were the lucky three." He smiled wickedly. The fire reflected off his face making him look as evil as he truly was. "Frances is clearly the weak link here, but she will do."

"Why me?" I asked, flashing back to our last conversation in his office. He thought I was powerful. Like everyone else foolishly thought. I rolled my eyes.

"You have potential, Ms. Parker, but there are things not even you know about yourself. Things witches have predicted. I can't have threats this close to me."

He turned his back to us and walked toward the fire. While he mumbled a spell, I saw Frances move slightly. She was slowly gaining consciousness. I looked over at Headmistress Craw, hopeful that she would also be waking up, but her head was still hung. He must have placed a slumber spell on her. He knew better than to allow her to wake up out here like this. Frances' face went from confusion to panic as her eyes peeled open. She blinked rapidly trying to figure out her position in the forest. She quickly realized she couldn't move her body and was now taped to a chair like me and Craw. A shrill noise escaped her throat. Not really a scream. Worse than that. It was like her body was on fire. She was in agony.

The sound caused Howard to stop his mumbling and turn his head in our direction. "Ah, you're awake already. That didn't take long." He turned swiftly, swinging his dark cape behind him, and crept toward Frances. She was still screaming when he stopped in front of her.

"Why? Wil, I love you!" she wailed at the top of her lungs. Tears streamed down her face and for the first time since I met her our first year, my heart ached for Frances. Professor Howard was unfazed. He simply lifted his finger to his mouth to shush her. Somehow, he was smiling while watching her lose her mind. When she saw his finger reach his mouth, she regained as much composure as she could. "Why?" she breathed. She wasn't screaming anymore, but nothing could stop her tears from coming.

"Why what?" he sighed like he was bored.

"Why am I tied up? Paralyzed?" Frances choked back a yelp.

"Oh, dear girl. What sort of sacrifice only has two victims? Honestly, your ignorance is almost adorable," he giggled. "Three is the magic number."

"You said you loved me," she mumbled, defeated, as she

realized there was nothing she could say to change his mind. He fooled her. Frances wouldn't survive this. She was a part of the planning. She knew what would happen next better than anyone. Professor Howard bent down and placed a light kiss on top of her head before returning to the fire. My stomach churned.

I racked my brain for a solution, thinking of every single spell I had learned in class, but I couldn't think of one powerful enough to take on the Underworld. People acted like I was such a strong witch. I scoffed at how wrong they had been. I couldn't save anyone. I cursed myself for not studying more on my own like Miles.

Miles. I would never see him again. I would never know what the rest of my life would have been like. *Our* lives. Would we have ended up together? At this moment, I felt certain we would have, but I would never know for sure. I hated Professor Howard for doing this to him. I was Miles' closest friend. We were family now. He had no mother. His father put up a wall when he decided to go to school here. He was mostly alone. Like me. My chest ached thinking of leaving him. The pain was almost intolerable. I dropped my head down and dry heaved.

I turned my attention to Frances to distract myself. She was panicked. Her head was twisting every direction, searching for a route of escape. But there was none. "Frances," I called out. "Breathe." I breathed slowly and dramatically in through my nose and out through my mouth so she would mimic my motions. She did, though her breaths came out shaking and her lips trembled. "It's okay," I tried to reassure her even though it wasn't true.

"This is not okay, Josie. None of this is okay. I'm so sorry." She hung her head. There was nothing I could say to comfort her. Soon we would be sacrificed, and I couldn't stop it. The numbness I forced myself to feel when I turned my face to stone had somewhat returned. I didn't feel scared. Just sad. Sad because I would miss so many things I spent my whole life dreaming of. Devastated because I would never marry Miles. Heartbroken because I would never see Lillian's purple eyes light up again. Hollow for all the witches we were leaving behind. The witches who would have their free will ripped away from them if all this actually worked. Perhaps we were lucky we wouldn't be on Earth for that.

"Headmistress Craw! Headmistress Craw! Please, wake up," Frances begged. Craw didn't move. "Dammit!" She tilted her head back and stared at the sky. "It's over, isn't it?" She was still looking up, her warm breath creating puffs of smoke in the cold air. I did not respond. Professor Howard's chanting was getting louder.

"Claricito daemonium gehennam ignis. Nostrorum potestatem unum." I recognized words like "demon" and "hellfire," but I couldn't understand the rest. I wasn't used to hearing spells *this* evil. I wasn't sure if I would be able to see the souls and demons that he called to Earth to help him, but I closed my eyes just in case. I didn't want that to be the last picture in my head. Instead, I imagined Miles. His eyes shone when he saw I would be sitting next to him on the first day of class this year. They were a clear blue that day. He shook my hand when he formally introduced himself. I thought of the Black Forest lit up in twinkling lights on our first date. The flowers that were still sitting beside my bed. The way he whispered he loved me at the dance. His hands on my waist. I imagined kissing him in ways I never had the chance to do.

Professor Howard's chanting grew incessantly louder, interrupting my perfect dreams. I still refused to open my eyes, but I heard Frances' shrill screech of terror. Had the monsters come for us? Professor Howard was yelling his chant now, and there was a certain pleasure in his voice. My heart started thumping in my chest. I repeated Miles' name over and over and over in my head until my mind was screaming it trying to drown out the noises around me. I heard the wails that didn't belong to anyone I knew. Cries from the dead. My mind took me back to the party I attended at Crystal's dorm room weeks ago. She had described this very scene. Her devil's juice potion allowed her to see this grim future. I shuddered.

I could not see—my eyes were still shut tight—but I

could feel the tension growing around me, swelling bigger and bigger, pushing down on my chest like a stone. It was hard to breathe. The air was steaming hot and for a second I was sure Hell had come to Earth. I sucked in as much air as I could, but it felt like my lungs were shrinking. *I'm going to suffocate.* I tried to drag thoughts of Miles' back into my mind, but the lack of oxygen was taking a toll.

I felt dizzy and was sure I was spinning in circles at an impossible speed. This was enough to force my eyes open, but when I looked, I was still in the same chair. I wasn't spinning. I couldn't see much except black spots in my vision, but I made out a figure in the corner of my eye. The figure was running towards us and suddenly two more figures appeared close behind the first.

They called my name. "Josie!" *No no no!* They were coming for me. The demons were coming to drag me to the Underworld. Professor Howard began chanting something new. Something in a language I never heard. It sounded nothing like the spells we learned in school.

I sealed my eyes shut again. "Josie!" the voice wailed. I was confused. This voice was too beautiful. More like an angel than a demon. I heard a groan and my eyes sprung back open. I saw, in front of me, Headmistress Craw's eyes were wide open. She was awake, frantic and clearly terrified, but she could help us. I tried to call out her name. I tried to move my lips to explain what was happening.

But it was too late. The dark spots in my vision kept growing until I was trapped in the darkness, unable to breathe.

"Josie!" the angel cried out.

Miles.

* * *

I had no idea what amount of time had passed. All I knew was that I felt safer than before. Professor Howard was still chanting by the fire, but he was screaming a defensive spell now, one I'd heard before, instead of the foreign tongue he was chanting in before. My vision was clear, and I could see the one thing I had imprinted in my mind since I realized I wouldn't make it out of the forest. Ice blue eyes burning into mine. But these eyes were worried, and it made me feel sad. Miles' arms were wrapped around me, cradling me. I was no longer in the chair, but on the forest floor. I wiggled my fingers and they moved. The paralysis spell was broken or had worn off. I wasn't sure which, but I didn't care because it meant I could touch his face. I put my hand on his cheek and felt the smooth skin I thought I would surely never feel under my fingertips again. He kissed my hand in quick spurts and relief flooded his face.

"You're okay?" he asked. I only nodded. Truthfully, I felt dizzy and weak, and blood was clouding my vision again. The cut must have split back open somehow. A nod was safer than trying to speak. I didn't want him to look worried anymore.

"Don't move. I will be right back." His arms slipped away from mine. I tried to reach for them again, but he was running. I was behind a tree, not far from the fire, but I couldn't see

Professor Howard anymore. I could only hear him. I turned my head to see where Miles was going. He stopped and grabbed Headmistress Craw's hand. She was standing facing the fire in a line with Lillian, Professor Rose, and a very weak looking Frances.

Lillian was awake! They had found us. My joy was short lived as I watched them straining against Professor Howard's power. They were calling on their ancestors for help. The forest air was thick, and I could sense the spirits of their families were there behind them. But I could also still feel the heat in the air, and I knew the demons from the Underworld were present, too. And they were not on our side.

Get up now, baby girl. I heard a voice in my head, but it wasn't mine. I hadn't heard this voice in years, but I recognized it immediately. My heart swelled. It was my mother's. I looked all around me. The only thing I saw were trees. My mother wasn't here. I laid my head back on the first floor, disoriented. *You must help them, Josie. You must fight for the light.* Maybe I had a concussion. Maybe Professor Howard's spells had made me lose my mind.

Or maybe my mother's spirit was really here, like the spirits of the other ancestors fighting on our side even though I hadn't called her. I had to listen, whether her voice was real or not. I got up slowly, using a tree for support. It was a strange sensation to be able to use my limbs again. I wiped the blood from my face. There was a lot of it. Once my vision was cleared, I started hobbling towards their line. I focused all my attention on Miles' hand. I must reach it. My movements were slower than I would have liked given the situation, but if I walked any faster, I was afraid I would fall over. My body had never felt so frail, but I had to listen to the voice. *That's right, baby girl. Keep going. Keep going.*

Miles' hand was right in front of mine. Just one more step and I would reach it. I lifted my foot to step over a fallen tree branch and grabbed his hand as tightly as I could. His head jerked sideways, and he saw me. It broke his focus, stopping him mid-spell. "Josie," he whispered. Losing his focus meant our line of defense lost his power and the power of his ancestors. The sky was suddenly darker. I looked up and saw no stars and the full moon had disappeared. The wind became violent, turning a small breeze into the beginning of a tornado. Professor Howard had the upper hand. I whipped my body forward to face him. His expression was joyous. He knew he would win, but as his eyes moved down the line his face began to change. When he saw me, my hand locked with Miles', his focus faltered. His smirk changed to something different. Doubt. Fear.

"Focus!" Headmistress Craw called. I threw myself into the spell. "Exillium infernum daemones!" The spell was unknown to me, but as soon as the words left my tongue, I felt their strength. We were banishing the Underworld from our realm. I pushed every piece of my body and mind into the spell. So much so that I knew I wouldn't be able to keep it up for long. I was too weak, and my body was dangerously close to toppling over. Professor Howard could see this, and his smirk returned. He continued with his defensive spell, and I knew if we couldn't defeat him his spell would be enough to kill us all. He would have more than enough sacrifices, more than enough power.

My vision was blurring, and my mouth was dry, but I forced the words out over and over. "Exillium infernum daemones! Exillium infernum daemones!" The wind was violent, and the fire raged. Tree branches began breaking off, crashing to the ground. I looked up and could see the tops of the trees, impossibly far in the sky, were waving back and forth. Leaves filled the air. I wondered how the trees were still standing at all. I chanted the spell for the tenth time, and I knew it would be my last. I was spent.

But suddenly the voice returned. I couldn't make out the exact words, but I could feel my strength returning. My ancestors were with me. My mother was with me. I could feel their power holding me upright. I no longer felt weak. I felt stronger than I ever had in my young life, power coursing through every fiber of my being. The wind howled and I heard a tree crash behind me. The air was cooling. We were winning.

You can do whatever you please if you have the right help. Professor Howard's own words rang clear in my head as I heard my mother's voice chanting with me. I closed my eyes and pictured her beside me. Her brown hair blew in the wind and her green eyes twinkled, and it felt like my mother had never left. In my mind, she looked as alive as she had the last morning she kissed me goodbye. I wondered if anyone else could tell her spirit was here. I opened my eyes to look at Professor Howard, and I had my answer. His face was pale, and his eyes were furious. He knew she was here. He could feel her presence. I closed my eyes and pictured her face again. The temperature dropped another degree.

Trees snapped behind us and I heard them crash, bringing other trees down with them. Professor Howard fell to his knees and the fire behind him no longer raged. It was dimming, losing its power, just like him. He stopped chanting and let out a tortured scream. He knew he would lose now. A branch, bigger than our whole line of defense, swung from a tree and struck his body, flinging him backwards. And in the blink of an eye it was over. The wind stopped, the fire disappeared, and the temperature dropped back down to normal. There was no longer a thickness in the air. It was easier to breathe. The demons and spirits were gone, all our connections to the great beyond broken, good and bad. But that meant my mother was gone, too. I looked over my left shoulder, searching for a sign that she was still here, but there was nothing. I only saw the destroyed forest behind me. All of us were silent and still for what seemed like a very long time.

It was me who broke the silence. Since my mother was gone, so was the strength she had lent me. My body was incredibly weak again and the sudden temperature drop sent me into small convulsions. I was so cold. "Miles," I whimpered. His arms were around me instantly, holding me up. Everyone was moving then. Lillian rushed to my side and wrapped her arms around me. Her motions were quick and wild. She ripped off her jacket and applied pressure to my head. They lowered me to the ground and Lillian's hands were moving rapidly, checking every part of my body.

"Are you hurt anywhere else?" she asked with tears in her eyes. I imagined it was just as difficult for her to see me on the ground this way as it was for me to see her in that hospital bed.

"I'm okay," I said in an attempt to calm them both even though it was far from the truth. My vision was going black again. I blinked hard to fight back against the darkness. *I will not pass out.*

"He's alive," I heard Professor Rose say. I looked to see her on the ground with Professor Howard's head in her lap. He was unconscious and the branch covered the lower half of his body. And I felt sad for her. If the rumors of her and Howard were true, how would she feel now? How did she feel fighting against him?

Headmistress Craw rushed over chanting "auferetur," and in one swift swoop of her arm the branch was lifted off of his body. "We need to get back to the school immediately." Her black dress was torn and dragged the ground, and her arms were stained with her own blood. She helped Professor Rose lift Howard and Miles scooped me off the ground. I pressed my head against his chest and relaxed a little.

The trek back seemed short, but that was thanks to my fading consciousness. I drifted in and out the whole time, only catching glimpses of the tops of the trees, a full moon, and, eventually, a terrified Mr. Dan sprinting from his guard shack, calling for help on his radio. The sight of Mr. Dan signaled something in my mind. I was safe. We were back. And my mind shut itself down.

14
SAFE AND SOUND

I woke up in a hospital bed. I realized quickly it was the same one Lillian had been in. It might have been alarming to most people to wake up here, but I had never felt more at ease. I was back at school. I survived.

I reached my hand to my eyes to wipe away whatever was making them stick together. It wasn't blood this time. I could tell my face had been cleaned. My eyelashes were matted together. I must have slept hard. How long was I out? I surprisingly slept a dreamless sleep. Maybe it was because of my head injury, or because I had been through a traumatic situation. I pulled the covers down and noticed my black dress was replaced by a hospital gown, and I had a needle in my arm with clear liquid traveling through a tube into my bloodstream. I glanced around to see I wasn't alone. Lillian was in the chair beside me with her eyes closed. She appeared to be asleep, so I stopped moving, not wanting to wake her. She was in different clothes than she had been in the forest. Obviously quite a bit of time *had* passed. My body felt sore and stiff, like I hadn't moved in a while. I lifted my hand up to check the wound on my head. All I could feel was a bandage.

I heard voices in the hall then and footsteps heading for my room. "He's been detained," Headmistress Craw explained. Her voice echoed down the empty hall. "He will be banished now. Howard won't be allowed to step foot on the island again. I will make sure of it."

"Are you positive he won't come back?" Miles asked anxiously. I could imagine his face coated with anxiety, his brow furrowed with worry. I frowned, longing for him to walk closer so I could stop his fretting.

"Yes. I am seeing to it myself," Craw reassured him. "The administration is not taking this lightly."

"Headmistress, I cannot express how sorry I am." It was Professor's Rose's soft voice speaking now. Regret stained every word. "If I would have had any idea, I--"

"Rose, please," Craw interrupted her. "None of this is your fault."

The three of them entered my room and stopped the conversation immediately when they saw I was awake. Miles rushed to my side. "Josie," he smiled. The company woke

Lillian. She looked around groggily until her eyes met mine. They shot open, the purple in them blazing, and she jumped up from her chair. I smiled. I had been so worried I would never see that purple again.

"Hey!" she said cheerfully. "How are you?" She lightly placed her hand on my shoulder and Miles intertwined his fingers with mine on the other side of the bed.

"I'm fine," I said, and I meant it. With the exception of some aches and stiffness, I felt as normal as I could expect to feel. "How are you, Headmistress Craw?" She wasn't in a hospital gown, but she had a bandage on her head to match mine.

"I am fine, Josie. Don't worry about me," she laughed. "The situation has been taken care of, too, so you don't need to worry about that either."

"I heard you guys talking in the hall," I admitted. "Is he really gone?"

"He will be tomorrow. He won't see another day of freedom," Craw said confidently.

"He won't...I mean...they aren't going to kill him, are they?" I asked, hesitantly, my eyes glancing in Professor Rose's direction. She was still standing in the doorway, keeping her distance. Her head was hung low and I could practically see the guilt weighing down her slumped shoulders. I didn't blame her, of course, if she wanted him to live. I didn't even want

Professor Howard to be executed. Not just for Professor Rose's sake. Even though he had almost killed us all, I couldn't justify taking a life. It didn't seem like the right thing to do after everything that happened tonight. We had to be better than that.

Headmistress Craw took one step closer to my bed. "No, dear. We will not put him to death, but he will not hurt you again." I felt relief and squeezed Miles' hand.

"What about Frances?" I asked, hesitantly.

Craw dropped her head and shook it. "We haven't had a student wrapped up in a mess of this caliber in many moons." I heard my heart rate increase on the monitor. They wouldn't banish her too, would they? I thought of her face in the forest as she paced with worry and regret, then as she reached for my ties to free me. I pictured how Howard spoke to her, with an exasperated tone. He was the one in control. Not Frances.

"Headmistress, it wasn't her fault," I couldn't stop the words from leaving my lips. "Truly. Professor Howard...he manipulated her. It was as if she was under a spell. She thought she could trust him. She thought she was following the Fallen Angel." I knew this would strike a chord with Craw since she had once been a devoted Follower herself. She did terrible things, too. And she was given a second chance. Craw raised her head and placed her hands on her hips. "She was scared, Headmistress. And she tried to save both of us before it was too late, but Howard knocked her out, too."

"Is that so?" Craw asked, seriously considering my words.

"Yes. She's not evil. She was just caught up in something bigger than herself." I had to stick up for Frances. I was the only one who had seen her guilt. She wasn't going to go through with it. I trusted she had good in her.

I felt Lillian stiffen beside me and my heart sank. Frances hurt her, too. And she had not been in the forest to see the power Howard had over her. I certainly didn't forgive Frances for nearly killing my best friend, but I needed to show mercy. I turned to look Lillian in the eyes. They were tight slits and I could barely see their color.

"I know she hurt you, too, Lillian. I'll explain everything, I promise." Lillian's eyes softened and she nodded. She trusted me. Once she heard exactly what I saw in the Black Forest, she would want to show Frances mercy, too, because no matter how angry we both were, we had to stand for what was right. And banishing Frances to a cell along with Professor Howard would not be right.

Headmistress Craw simply nodded her head before turning to leave the room. She looked back over her shoulder before exiting. "I think you're right, Ms. Parker. I will keep it in mind when deciding her punishment." She slid by Professor Rose and I heard her heels clicking down the hall. Even after a near death experience, she still managed to wear heels.

Professor Rose stepped forward next and stood at the foot of my bed. She looked down at the floor as she spoke. "Josie, you have no idea how sorry I am. I was close with Professor Howard. Very close." So, the rumors were true. Not only did Howard make Frances believe he loved her, he fooled Rose into thinking the same. That couldn't have been an easy task, and I shivered thinking of how manipulative Howard must be. "However, I had no idea about any of this." She lifted her gaze from the floor and looked me in the eyes as she said the next words. "I would never allow *anyone* to put you in harm's way."

"I know that, Professor," I assured her. She stepped back and ran her hands down the front of her baby blue dress like she was trying to straighten out wrinkles even though there were none.

"Thank you, Josie. You are very gracious." She stepped back and looked at Lillian and Miles on either side of me. "Well, I will give you three some privacy. We will speak soon." She exited the room and we listened as her footsteps disappeared.

"How long was I out?" I asked, looking at Miles and squeezing his hand lightly.

"Just over 24 hours," he said, choking out the words as if they burned his throat.

"What about Frances? How is she?" Lillian's face twisted

into a look of confusion and slight frustration. She still didn't understand how I could defend Frances. Part of me didn't understand either. But I couldn't help but remember how Professor Howard described Frances in the forest. "Someone desperate for love and approval. Someone who could be manipulated, who could be blamed if things went wrong. Frances was just the right girl." Miles worked hard to keep his face neutral as he answered. His sympathy for Frances was also limited.

"She's in the next room over," he snarled. He was angry with her, just like Lillian.

"How do you feel?" I asked Lillian to change the subject.

"I'm fit as a fiddle. All healed." She held out her arms, then shrugged. "Now we just have to get *you* better."

"How did you know? How did you find us?" I asked them.

"I woke up sometime during the dance. I was confused at first and couldn't remember how I ended up there, but then it all hit me like a ton of bricks. Everything that happened in the library. Everything I heard Professor Howard say. He planned to use you as a sacrifice the whole time. I knew I had to get to you. So, I screamed bloody murder for a nurse, and we got Professor Rose. On our way out we ran into Miles." She looked up at Miles and smiled sympathetically. "The poor boy was running the halls searching for you. He was in total panic mode. I told him what I knew, and we headed for the forest out the back door. We made it just in time, too. His sacrifice was almost complete..." Her voice drifted and despair filled her eyes. I imagined she was thinking of what would have happened if they had been too late.

"What exactly happened in the library?" I asked. I never heard the full story.

"I was looking for a book for class. The librarian told me it was towards the back. I was in a section I never even knew existed. I thought for sure I would be alone back there, but I heard voices. They were talking about...awful things. I was scared so I started to leave, but then I heard your name. So, I walked closer. I held my breath the whole time while they laid out their plan. Howard admitted to killing the young girl. They said you and Headmistress Craw would be their sacrifices in the Black Forest. Everything. That's when Howard told Frances she had to kill someone, too, if she wanted to prove her loyalty. I turned to run, but I think Professor Howard had already seen me. Or heard me. That's why he told Frances she had to kill someone. He was talking about me." She shivered beside me. "And that was it. I'm not sure what Frances did, but the last thing I remember is her voice whispering." It was easy to let the anger take over me when I heard her spiel. Easy to think horrible things about Frances. She probably deserved some of them. But I fought hard to stop myself. This was all Howard's fault. Frances showed her true colors in the Black

Forest. Though she redeemed herself at least a little, it still wasn't easy to push back the dark thoughts after hearing what she had done to my best friend.

I held out my arms to Lillian, and she curled her tiny body in them, climbing fully on the bed. "Ever since Mom died you've always tried to take care of me. I wish I had been there to take care of you this time." Tears fell down my face before I even realized I was crying. Once they started, they were impossible to stop. It was understandable that my emotions were out of whack. I had almost lost my best friend, been poisoned, nearly sacrificed, and heard my mother's voice all within the span of a few days. "I'm sorry," I sobbed. "I can't stop crying." I'd never felt so many things at the same time.

"It's okay, darling," Miles comforted me, wiping the tears off my face. I looked over to see Lillian had tears streaming down her face, too. "It's normal to have an emotional reaction after you've performed a spell of that magnitude. That alone could send you over the edge. I haven't felt normal either, and I didn't go through half of what you ladies did. You're both so brave." He bent down and kissed my wet cheek. "I love you, Josie."

"I love you, too." I pulled his face towards mine to kiss him and Lillian sat straight up in the bed.

"Wait, what did you just say?" she gawked. "Did I just hear the word *love*?" It occurred to me that I hadn't gotten the chance to tell her. She stared at me with her mouth wide open, and my tears stopped. A blush spread across my face and Lillian squealed. "Tell me everything!" She crawled to the end of the bed and crossed her legs and put her chin in her hands, waiting patiently for me to begin. So, I told her everything. All about the night we first said, "I love you," the dance, the punch, the Black Forest, and finally how Frances tried to save me. When I finished, it felt like a weight was lifted from my chest. It was over. I had my best friend back, sitting on the end of my bed, and the love of my life in a chair beside me, holding my hand. I felt whole.

15
WINTER BREAK

I laid on my bed and watched Lillian stuff her suitcase full. It was the first semester break at North End, and Lillian was packing to spend our week off with her family in Italy. Some of her clothes were sprawled on my bed, while the others were either crumpled on her closet floor or being squished into her suitcase.

"You know you'll only be gone like six days, right?" I asked, even though I knew my words meant nothing. She did this every time we had a break.

"I'm just excited! Plus, we're having a huge family dinner one night and I don't know what I'll want to wear, but I know I want to be the most stylish cousin at the dinner. So, I need plenty of options." She pushed both her hands down on the pile of clothes in an attempt to make room for two more dresses. I rolled my eyes and laughed. Only Lillian would be worried about being the most stylish at a family dinner.

I rolled on my back and stared at my closet. I had no clothes sprawled across the floor, no suitcase to pack. I was staying here this winter break. It had only been four short weeks since the night in the Black Forest and traveling home to see my dad sitting silently in his chair was more than I could handle at the moment. I reach up to rub the scar on my head, the only physical proof that Hallow's Eve had truly happened. I hadn't needed stitches, but the gash had only fully healed a week ago. I rolled back over to see Lillian still struggling with her suitcase.

I hopped off the bed to offer my assistance. Once she had the last two dresses in the suitcase, I pressed down on the top as hard as I could while she zipped it closed. "There! It fits," she beamed. "Barely, but it works." She dashed across the room to shove a few more small items into the oversized purple purse I had gotten her for her birthday last year. It was the same shade as her eyes.

I tried to smile while Lillian ran back and forth across the room remembering last minute items she wanted to pack, but it was difficult. I couldn't help but feel a little jealous of her. Her family always got together this time of the year, and when she returned, she would have a glow on her face that only came from the kind of happiness you get when you spend time with your bloodline. It was the same thing I used to feel when I took family trips. I wanted to be happy for her. I *was* happy for her, but watching her excitement only reminded me that I would never have that again. I turned my attention to my nails, looking down and pushing my cuticles back to distract myself. Lillian must have noticed because she stopped what she was doing to flop down beside me.

"You can still come with me you know? We have plenty of room and I can get your plane ticket no problem." She had already extended this offer twice before, but I declined each time. I loved Lillian and her family, but I was certain that seeing them all together would only make me feel empty. Lillian was just as close with her mother as I had been with mine and seeing their bond was painful.

"I appreciate the offer. Really, I do, but Miles is staying back so he will keep my company." She didn't look convinced, so I widened my smile until I knew I looked ridiculous. "Seriously! Look!" I said through my teeth. Lillian laughed half-heartedly.

"Please, call me," she said before shoving her suitcase off the bed. It landed with a thump. I had no idea how she was going to handle that thing on a ferry ride *and* through an airport. It was almost as big as her.

"You sure you can carry that?" I asked hesitantly.

"Yep," she grunted as she used her weight to flip it over.

"It has wheels." She pulled up the handle with ease and started rolling towards the door.

"Be safe, please," I said. She stopped suddenly, whirled around, and ran in my direction. I stood and we wrapped our arms around each other, holding on tightly. "I love you, best friend." I felt a lump rising in my throat. I knew it was ridiculous. It was just a week, but it was the first time since Hallow's Eve that we would be apart.

"I love you, too. So much." She gave me one final squeeze before heading back to her suitcase. "Seriously. Call me. And have fun with your *boyfriend*." She practically sang the word "boyfriend" and winked at me before opening the door. I over-exaggerated my eye roll before she rolled her suitcase into the hallway and closed the door behind her.

I plopped back down on my bed and stared at the ceiling for only a moment before I decided it was too quiet. Ava and Daliah had already left to head back home for the break, and the silence was so loud it was ringing in my ears. I picked up my phone and dialed Miles. He answered on the first ring. "Hey, are you busy?" I asked.

"Nope. My roommates just left so I'm pretty much just staring at the ceiling," he sighed.

"Same. It's too quiet."

"Do you want to come over?" he asked. "I rented a few movies from the library. You can pick which one to watch."

"Yes, please. I'll be over in a few." I started to pull the phone away from my ear to hang up when I heard Miles nearly yell.

"Wait!" he called. I put the phone back up to my ear. "I'll just come get you. I don't want you to walk alone." Ever since *that* night, Miles had been overprotective. He walked me to all of my classes, with the exception of the ones I had with Lillian, since he knew Lillian would accompany me. If I wanted to grab a snack from the café, he made sure he was there waiting for me. We barely spent an hour away from each other in four weeks if you didn't count bedtimes and classes. He started looking after Lillian, too. We basically became the three musketeers. I was worried I would feel suffocated or would get sick of him or he would get sick of me or that Lillian would get angry that he was around all the time, but it had the opposite effect. Lillian and Miles were already becoming close friends and she loved the way he looked after me. I did, too. He knew I could fend for myself, but he never wanted me to feel afraid again.

However, I knew he could not always be at my side to make me feel comfortable. "I think I'll walk alone this time," I said. The silence on the other end let me know he was uneasy with the idea. "Listen, it has to happen eventually. I can't always have you and Lillian as bodyguards." I laughed and heard him laugh on the other end.

"Okay. If you're sure…"

"I'm sure. Plus, Headmistress Craw kept guards in most of the hallways. I'll be fine," I said partially to reassure him and partially to reassure myself. "I'll see you in five minutes." I hung up the phone and grabbed my blue, oversized sweater that was hanging on the end of my bed and wrapped it around myself. The temperature dropped significantly the past few weeks. It was chilly 43 degrees today.

I walked down the halls slowly, trying to be aware of my surroundings, but not obsessed with looking over my shoulder. It was a delicate balance. The first week after the incident I was jumpy, to say the least. Every little noise scared me, and I woke up in a cold sweat from nightmares of a dark hooded figure every single night for 12 days straight. I hated it. It made me feel weak and vulnerable. Lillian was nervous, too, but it hadn't had the same effect on her. It was taking me longer to recover from it all.

However, after those 12 days were over my attitude changed. The nightmares slowed and no longer came every night. I still looked over my shoulders, but the paranoia was slowing down, too. Instead, I was learning to appreciate my surroundings while being acutely aware of them. I saw beauty in the castle I had never seen before. I noticed people. I smiled at girls in my hall and struck up conversations with witches in my classes I had never taken the time to speak to before. I was coming out of my shell a little, and it was a surprisingly glorious feeling. I was still somewhat shy and quiet. I loved that about myself, but I was changing in ways I loved, too.

The halls were silent as I glided through them. Most students went out of town for the break, but I did pass a few witches walking alone in the halls. Not everyone had wonderful families to return to. So, Miles and I wouldn't be completely alone on campus this week. I passed two first year students in Miles' hall and they both turned to whisper to each other as they passed me. Most people didn't even try to hide the fact that they were talking about me. The first two weeks I was the talk of the school, along with everyone else who was involved. Heads turned every single time we walked into a room and whispers soon followed. That was another reason I started talking to more people. If they were going to talk about me, I wanted them to know the *real* me. Not the me that their friends painted as they gossiped about the latest island scandal. Ava had been right, though. People didn't have much else to do on this island besides talk. And that's exactly what they did.

Lillian, Miles, Professor Rose, Headmistress Craw, and I were painted as heroes in most of the stories, while Professor Howard and Frances were cast as villains. But every now and then I would hear a story about how I was also helping Professor Howard. Some people didn't find the original story interesting enough. Near death experiences must not have entertained them for long so they made up details. Like I had been involved with Professor Howard the same way Frances had. They pitted Frances and I against each other in these tales, as if we were fighting over him. Ridiculous. Thankfully, not many people believed that account. Even the first year students seemed to know it made no sense.

A part of me felt sad for Frances when I heard the talk around school. Not a single story had any remorse or understanding for her, not even the made-up ones. People didn't realize she had been a victim in her own way. They liked forgetting the part where she tried to save me and only mentioned that she was sleeping with a professor and had become a Follower, which I wasn't even sure was true anymore. Frances was still enrolled at school, but I hadn't seen her since she visited me in the hospital ward.

The night after I woke up, she came to talk to me. She apologized over and over, saying she knew that didn't make it right, but that she still had to say it. I'd never seen her that way. She was completely vulnerable, unafraid to show her regret. Lillian had been there, too, and she apologized to her, as well.

"I don't expect forgiveness," she said to the two of us. "I don't deserve it. I let Professor Howard take over every piece of me. I was not strong enough." She explained that she had a lot of issues to sort through on her own and that she was trying to be a better person. She even told us she planned to learn more about the Divinity before surrendering her whole life to some force she barely knew anything about. The rumors never mentioned this side of Frances. I couldn't blame most people, though. Frances had practically dubbed herself as a villain before any of this even happened. People were basing this off the facade Frances put on in front of them all these years. They only knew her as the girl that snarled at them in the halls for no apparent reason.

Even though she hadn't asked for our forgiveness, we both gave it, though Lillian more begrudgingly. Not just for her sake, but for our own. Living the rest of our lives with a grudge seemed unpleasant. So, we forgave her and told her we would be there to help her along the way if she needed us. I knew Frances had kindness somewhere in her heart. She just needed to stop thinking that was a weakness.

I'd heard Frances was on a strict probation. She wasn't allowed to attend classes in person until Headmistress Craw said otherwise, and she had been moved out of her room to a private dorm in a small wing of the castle that housed troubled students. Counseling was available 24/7 there and her classes were online. If she stayed on the right track, she would be able to slowly return to regular classes, but she would remain under strict probation for the remainder of her years at North End. This included curfews, random check ins from the Headmistress and guards, and separate housing in the small, monitored wing of the school. Eventually, she would be able to leave this whole mess behind her though. We only had two and a half years until graduation. Then we would all be free to go anywhere and do anything we pleased. As much as I was looking forward to that time, I imagined Frances even more excited.

I pushed open Miles' door without knocking and ran straight for him, jumping in his arms and wrapping legs around his waist. I pushed my lips against his, hard, and tangled his hair in my hands. He kissed me back lightly, but something was off. His lips were tight and hesitant. I pulled away and looked at his face. It was stone. I released my legs from his waist and hopped down to my feet.

"What's wrong?" I asked and wondered when my heart would stop dropping to my stomach every time the smallest thing seemed off.

"Well…" Miles gaped at an opened envelope in his hand and stayed silent. This wasn't something small. No. If it was something that could be easily fixed, then Miles would have explained it right away. Instead he stayed quiet, his eyes fixed on the envelope.

"What is that?" I asked, fighting against the urge to rip it from his hands and look at it myself. He slowly held it up in front of my face. It was very wrinkled, like he had crumpled it up in his hand and tried to straighten it out again. Miles' name and the school's address were etched in the center, but there was no return address.

A sick feeling began turning in my stomach. I somehow knew who it was from, but I could not stop myself from asking again. "What is that?" My voice was devoid of any emotion.

"It's a letter," Miles answered. "From my mom."

ABOUT THE AUTHOR

A Morehead State University graduate from Hagerhill, KY, **AMANDA JADE TURNER** plays a middle school English teacher by day, and moonlights as a rock star by night.

When she's not molding young minds or making crowds swoon, she enjoys rewatching *The Office* on repeat, writing YA novels, and playing with her two dogs: Wilco and Lola.

North End: The Black Forest is her first novel.

.

CPSIA information can be obtained
at www.ICGtesting.com
Printed in the USA
LVHW110959201020
669267LV00023B/201/J

9 780998 219073